A Fight for Survival

By Ryker Holmgren

Edited By: Ailene Edits

Cover Art By: Hannah Nipko

All rights reserved

The characters and events portrayed in this book are fictitious. Any similarity to real persons, living or dead, is coincidental and not intended by the author.

No part of this book may be reproduced, or stored in a retrieval system, or transmitted in any form or by any means, electronic, mechanical, photocopying, recording, or otherwise, without express written permission of the publisher.

ISBN: 9798721468124

Imprint: Independently published

Authors Note

Throughout our lives we have been taught about the fight or flight response.

In moments of self-preservation the natural instinct is to flight, to flee, to run away.

I am sure in your life you have experienced this sensation.

You may also have witnessed someone, you thought you could count on, quit on you in a moment you could barely keep your head above water. You were left to realize you were going to face this trial alone.

This book is not about hunting. It is about a choice between fight or flight.

This is witnessing what someone is made of when the chips are down.

Will someone run in fear? Or could they truly have someone depend on them in a life-or death situation?

I hope that as you read. You place yourself in someone else's shoes.

What are YOU made of?

Could YOU truly stand in the fire and not blink?

Contents

Chapter 1: A Frightening Obsession 1
Chapter 2: Twenty Years Later 20
Chapter 3: The Night Before 27
Chapter 4: Preparing to Leave 39
Chapter 5: The Last of Civilization 49
Chapter 6: Into the Backcountry 59
Chapter 7: Early to Rise 79
Chapter 8: The Hunt Begins 90
Chapter 9: The Cabin 105
Chapter 10: Don't Look Back 119
Chapter 11: Being Pursued 130
Chapter 12: What Just Happened? 143
Chapter 13: Starting at the Bottom 152
Chapter 14: On the Trail 161
Chapter 15: Tracking 170
Chapter 16: Don't Move 178
Chapter 17: The Journey Out 194
Chapter 18: Making a Plan 205
Chapter 19: The Journey into Hell 215
Chapter 20: Never Give Up 224
Chapter 21: End of the Road 232

Chapter 1

A FRIGHTENING OBSESSION

It was a cool October morning. Flint could feel a slight chill on his skin as a soft breeze blew through the open widows. Car after car drove past as he sat on the side of the road, waiting in his truck to continue refinishing the asphalt. A heavy aroma of coffee filled the cab, though it barely covered the stink of dozens of empty tobacco cans behind his seat. He took a drink from his mug.

The radio crackled, "We're stopping traffic so you can come up and make your next pass," one of the other workers said.

Flint shifted the truck into first gear. As he drove around the stopped traffic, he noticed a worker turn to another and say something. *It's probably something about me,* Flint thought to himself. People were always talking about him behind his back, but he had learned to find the humor in it. He took another sip of coffee and flipped the switch to start spreading the oil.

As he drove back past his coworkers, he began to chuckle and roll his eyes. This was nothing new for Flint. He had been in middle school when he realized how creepy and intimidating the other kids thought he was at times. The children had all pushed him away, none of them realizing why he was that way. No one took the time to realize why Flint was that way. Even the teachers had pushed him off and out of their way, not bothering to investigate into his life just a little more. It had started at home, and Flint was just carrying the foundation he had formed there.

His dad hadn't been around much growing up, having bounced around the oil fields for work. Flint hadn't minded though, considering the man was a heavy drinker off the job and had always ended up being drunk at home. Because of the drink, anytime Flint had done something slightly wrong, he got beaten. Sometimes it hadn't even taken that, his father had often beaten him just to beat him, justifying the abuse by saying that he wasn't going to raise a wimp.

Flint turned up the truck's radio; it was playing a cassette tape of country music. Every time he realized people were talking about him, it would take him back to when people first started spreading rumors about him. Due to the way he grew up, Flint had rather enjoyed treating other people the way he had been treated at home. It had started as taking out his frustrations at his home life on others. Then it morphed to the point where he had just enjoyed hurting people. It hadn't taken long for the others to know it, too.

When Flint was fourteen, his dad had taken him on his first deer hunt. Right away, Flint had been shocked that his dad would take him to do something. His whole life his dad had told him how worthless he was, but now Flint finally got to go with him and be a part of something. They had planned to meet up with all his dad's friends at camp. His dad had started drinking immediately after turning off the highway, throwing beer can after beer can out the window. By the time they reached the camp site, he was already well on his way to being drunk, which meant he fit right in with the other men at the camp.

Getting out of the truck, the first thing his dad did was throw the tent at him. "Get to work and prove you're worth something," his father shouted.

Flint took the tent over to a clear spot and began setting up their camp while his father and his friends kept drinking.

It didn't take long for the men to become belligerent. "I told you guys that kid would be good for something." His dad threw and empty can at Flint, "Hey boy! Get me another beer!" he yelled at him.

The men soon pulled out their guns, waving them around and swinging the muzzles to point them at each other time and again. Then each of them would say how they were going to outdo the others, bragging about how they were going to bring home the biggest deer, though Flint thought it was doubtful any of them had shot a deer in

the last decade. The later the night got, the more vulgar and violent their stories became.

When that first the morning came, no one was in a hurry to wake up. Late in the morning — almost afternoon — Flint's father had grabbed him out of his sleeping bag and dragging him on a hike. His father had been extremely loud and clumsy. He had also reeked of alcohol. Flint was hiking ten yards behind him, and he could still smell the stale beer. His father was extremely out of shape and they never made it far from camp. He could tell that his father was just aimlessly roaming around the woods with no idea what he was doing.

That night, when they got back to camp, it was just more of the same. More beer, more stories, and more trash talk. The men just continued to make complete fools out of themselves. Flint sat back behind the fire watching and listening until the men were all passed out in random places around the camp. That's when he made his way to the tent and went to sleep.

When Flint woke the next morning, the men were still passed out, and the camp stunk of vomit and sour beer. The men had spent the whole second day moaning about how bad their heads hurt. Anytime someone made a sound, Flint could see the pain shoot through each man's head before someone would yell, "Keep it down, damn it! "They shifted around a bit, but none of them went anywhere that day. Flint had been left to sit around the camp, listening to them yelling at him all day.

By the time the third and final day of the trip had come, all Flint could think was that this shit show was finally coming to an end. He could almost go home. Because the men had spent the entire previous day recovering, they woke up almost early that day. There was a chill to the morning air, leaving a light frost on the ground. As they left camp for the trip's first hunt, the beer smell coming from Flint's father had gone completely stale. Every time the wind blew, it brought that stench toward Flint. He had to cover his mouth and nose to keep his body from heaving.

With the way his father randomly wondered around the woods, Flint could tell he knew nothing about hunting. For his father, the whole trip had been about nothing more than getting out in the woods so that he could be a bigger piece of trash then he already was. His father was sweating heavily, filling the air with his rancid stench of beer, when he stopped, setting down his rifle, and bent over, his hands braced on his knees, gasping for air. *This is my dad*, Flint thought to himself, looking on with complete shame.

Flint looked around as he waited for his father to recover, but he didn't have a clue what he was doing or what he was looking for. That's when he saw it, as his father was still bent over gasping for air.

Straight in front of them, not a hundred yards away, a small buck walked out from behind a tree. Flint stared at it for a few moments before alerting his dad, "Dad, dad there's a deer."

His farther looked up in complete shock before fumbling around with his rifle, struggling to get it shouldered and catch his breath. He finally gained control. *Crack!* With the smell of burnt gun powder in the air, the deer hit the ground.

They both immediately raced to the downed animal. "See, son, that's how it's done!" His father crowed, bragging about himself.

Flint let all that go in one ear and out the other as a different feeling came over him. The hair on his neck began to stand on end. A warming sensation spread through his body. He became more and more fascinated with the dying animal, paying close attention to the blood draining from it like a light stream of water from a faucet, and the body lying there, fighting for just a little more life. He knelt, running his hand across the body. The rough and scratchy hide of the deer pressed against his palm. He was surprised with how rough the hairs felt. It thrilled him to feel the small final twitches of the deer's nerves. Turning, he peered into the animal's dull eyes, watching the last signs of life fade away. A dark smile grew on his face.

Flint finished another pass on the road, noticing his truck was empty. He pulled away to fill the tank back up and take a lunch. He made his way to the break trailer and, once inside, to the same spot to eat as he did every day. It was far in the back corner of the room where he could be alone. In fact, Flint couldn't remember the last time he hadn't eaten alone.

Looking around the room, everyone had their lunches out. Sodas, candies, and greasy foods were the norm among the crew. Flint, however, ate quite healthy, aside from his cup of coffee in the morning and his chew, and he tried to stay in peak physical condition since watching his dad gasping for air during that hunting trip. His grooming standard wasn't quite the same, though. He maintained a grungy look everywhere he went. His beard was long and unkempt, his hair was almost to his shoulders and seemed to be greasy enough to ring the oil right out of it. So, it might have been a combination of his grooming and his irregular meal, but just like every other day, he sat alone for lunch and was left to think.

It hadn't been a year after his father took him hunting that his dad was killed in a drunk driving accident. When he found out, Flint tried to comfort his mother. For as much of a deadbeat as his father had been, his mother was still very grief stricken. Flint, however, was glad he would never have to deal with his father again. In the end, Flint had truly hated the man. His mother was a good woman though.

People in the community always wondered why she had never left Flint's father. It didn't take long for them to realize she had been browbeaten into submission. Even in death he hadn't left Flint's mother with much of anything, so the community stepped in and tried to help with money and raising Flint. But for as much as they tried, by fourteen his father's bad habits had already taken hold.

There was one family in the community though; Flint remembered them very well. The father's name was Ryan. Ryan was former military and always tried to bring the lessons the military had taught him to his family. Ryan had grown up living a very tough life and joining the military had given him a second chance. Not letting it pass him by, he had used it to turn his life around. At heart, Ryan was a family man and very caring. Flint could remember back to when Ryan first learned of Flint's father's death. Honestly, it felt like a glimmer of hope for the first time in Flint's dark life. Ryan had wanted to give the kid a chance. He had told Flint that he had thought back to his own experience, as well as knowing many others who had turned their lives around and hadn't wanted to leave Flint behind. After knowing how Flint's father was, Ryan knew flint never truly got a fair chance growing up. He wanted to give Flint that chance.

There was a local fishing spot that Ryan took his wife and kids every Sunday. With all their activities, Ryan always pushed to make sure his kids knew how important family was. Ryan had heard through his own kids that Flint had become infatuated with hunting. Being as Ryan was what most people would call an extreme outdoorsman, he invited Flint to go fishing with his family for the first time.

Flint didn't know the first thing about fishing. He spent the whole time cursing and using vulgar language around Ryan's family. Ryan had a son and a daughter about the same age as Flint, and they had tried to tell their dad not to bring Flint along. Ryan's children explained how much everyone at school stayed away from him. How it was just a waste of time to try and help him. Ryan could tell that Flint was a very troubled young man and took his time to work with him. Ryan knew it wasn't going to be an easy task. He would need a lot of patience to work with Flint. And even though his children didn't want Flint there, Ryan spent the afternoon with all of them, working, teaching, and explaining. By the end of the day, Flint was really starting to get the hang of things. Through multiple trips with them, Flint slowly became accustomed to being with Ryan's family. By then, even Ryan's kids didn't mind being around him so much anymore. Ryan taught his children and Flint the fundamentals of being in the outdoors, using every opportunity to teach them skills in everything they did.

That summer, Ryan tried to make Flint feel like a part of his family by taking him under his wing. Around Ryan's family Flint became a very decent and well-mannered kid. There were a few times he would revert to his old habits, but overall he had come leaps and bounds from where he had been before.

As the summer went on, Ryan would go about town and hear about how much trouble Flint had been in or how bad of a kid that Flint was. People would continuously ask Ryan why he was taking the time to help Flint, saying that he was beyond help. And every time, Ryan defended Flint by telling them that he wasn't a bad kid, he just got a bad rap and needs some good people to take some time to work with him. What Ryan didn't know was that all those old habits of Flint's father were still there, Flint just made sure to hide them when he was in front of Ryan or around his family. Flint was learning to manipulate his environment very well.

When fall came, Flint bought his first deer tag. After spending all summer working with Flint, Ryan felt that it would be good to take Flint hunting with them. As the weeks lead up to the hunt, Ryan took some extra time with Flint, teaching him about hunting a big game animal. He told Flint about how animals can pick up on sounds not found in nature and to always be careful of his clothes or pack dragging on sticks and branches. One night, Ryan was helping Flint work on his shooting. Flint slammed the safety forward. The click didn't ring any louder than normal, but Ryan found it as a good teaching point, explaining to Flint that at the range the click from the safety wasn't a big deal, but in the woods, the sound of that click would echo all around him. If a deer were close, it would easily pick up on the sound.

As they loaded up for the hunt, Flint could tell that Ryan's family did things completely different from his father. They made sure to take all the gear they needed in case of emergency; they were prepared for almost every scenario that they could come across. Ryan said it was better to have the gear and not need it, than need it and not have it. On the way to their hunting location, they passed hundreds of other hunters like Flint's father. They eventually found a place to pull off the road, and, looking around, Flint couldn't figure out where they would camp. Ryan soon explained that they would hike into the mountains and set up a spike camp a few miles into the woods.

Once they reached their camping area, they began to set up for the next few days. It wasn't much. The rest of the day they spend getting their tents, cooking, and a place for the fire set up. They had packed in everything they would need. It may have been just a spike camp, but they wanted to make it as comfortable as they could.

That night, Flint knew that Ryan saw the first sign of a red flag about him. Ryan made sure to gather the family around the fire, using the time to talk to his wife and children. Ryan never wanted to miss an opportunity to become closer with his family. This was the first moment when Flint's old bad habits began to show again around Ryan's family. Flint became vulgar, and it didn't take long for him to start to emulate his father's behavior. To Flint, this was the time to revert to what he knew. Multiple times, Ryan had to step in and cut off whatever Flint was talking about. Eventually, Ryan was able to get a handle on Flint. That wasn't the end of the red flags for the night though, because Flint began to talk about his excitement for the hunt to start.

    Ryan's kids always talked about how excited they were to go out hunting, but it was in a much different manner than Flint's. The way Ryan had taught his children was that hunting was a chance to have another adventure in the mountains with good people and a way to provide food for the family. Flint, on the other hand, had been taught differently. Flint kept talking about how excited he was to kill something, about how he was going to take the life of the deer. Ryan kept trying to interject, saying that hunting is about much more than just killing an animal, it's about spending time with people you care about and the enjoyment of being out in nature. He tried everything he could to explain to Flint that shooting an animal was an extremely small part of what they were going to be doing. But as much as Ryan tried to get this point a cross to Flint, Flint just kept coming back to wanting to kill something.

Finally, Ryan had to just stop Flint from talking. He told Flint to focus on the fire. To focus on the light in the dark. Ryan said that if he focused on the light, it would bring him warmth and comfort, even in his loneliest and most frightened times. Then Ryan told him to look up and turn around. To peer into the darkness that was in the woods around him. "What makes people afraid of the darkness?" Ryan asked.

Flint shrugged, "It's what you can't see. It's not that you're afraid cause your alone, it's that you're afraid you're not alone."

Ryan told Flint to turn back to the fire. "Now, look here in the light to where you want to be. Warm. Comforted. Able to see all the people you care about around you," Ryan said.

Flint looked at Ryan, rolling his eyes as he stood up, leaving the family around the fireside for his tent.

The next morning, everyone was ready well before daylight, wanting to get a good start. They wanted to be in their over watch spots before the sun was up. This way, they would be able to get a wide view with their optics, hoping to get to see the deer on their way to feed. All the kids were calm and collected, except for Flint, he was extremely eager. Ryan tried to bring back the habits that he had taught Flint throughout the summer, reminding him that he needed to have patients. Throughout the day, Ryan and his kids taught Flint even more things about hunting. They showed him how to check and work the wind so that the animals wouldn't smell him and how to spot important differences in tracks. Flint began to see how things worked in an efficient hunting party.

A day or two had passed on the mountain, and Ryan had all the kids up at their glassing points, keeping a close eye on a few bucks. They waited there in the dark until the sun began to rise. Ryan was sitting with Flint that morning and, once they were able to see, they noticed a heard of about twenty or so deer eating. The heard was at the bottom of the hill they were sitting on. The deer had just walked out of a group of trees and bushes to a small clearing of grass. As the morning got brighter, they were able to make out the bucks in the heard. Looking through the optics, Ryan helped steer Flint to the most mature buck in the group. It was plenty big, and Flint's breathing began to increase rapidly, and his arms began to shake. "Hey, Ryan, I think I can make that shot," Flint whispered.

"No, we need to make sure it's the right shot. I think I can get you closer. We need to take our time here," Ryan whispered back. Knowing that Flint wasn't an experienced shooter, Ryan moved him farther down the mountain.

Flint stopped multiple times to check to see if he could try and take a shot. And each time, Ryan stopped Flint, showing him how to move closer and stock the game. Even with his eagerness to shoot early, Flint was overtaken with fascination. It took them hours to get into position, but finally, they were there. Roughly two hundred yards out, Ryan had Flint set up for the shot. Flint perched his rifle on a rock, and Ryan helped him start to control his breathing. Once he was completely set up, Flint took his first breath in and slowly out, then a second breath. Flint slowly released the air out of his lungs on his third breath, and his aim steadied. *Crack!* The gun recoiled into Flint's shoulder causing him to lose sight on the deer. By the time he readjusted to look through the scope again, the entire herd had scattered and disappeared back into the trees. Except one. There was one deer left that laid flat on the ground.

"What a shot! See what patience can do? "Ryan shouted out.

Ryan's voice was ecstatic, but Flint didn't hear any of this. He wasn't thinking about anything Ryan had taught him about hunting. It was as if everything around him had gone completely silent. He wasn't focused on respecting the life of the deer or about the food he had just acquired. His mind turned away from anything he had been taught of how hunting should be. The only focus he had was that he had just taken a life.

They made their way to the fallen deer. Looking back, this is when Flint realized that Ryan started to change his interaction with him. Flint knew that Ryan had watched as his whole demeanor had changed and that it was at that moment that Ryan noticed what everyone had been warming him about. Flint didn't seem to care about getting congratulated or the success of the hunt, he was just happy to watch the animal die. Flint's eyes glazed over, and what Ryan would later call a sadistic smile spread across his face.

Flint wasn't concerned about anything other than the enjoyment of killing something, and Ryan could see it. In the time Ryan had spent in the military, he had seen looks like this before. He had seen men snap, losing their minds and giving into evil. Everyone of them had had that same look. It was the look of complete madness. Once he saw it on a man, there was no changing it. The most terrifying part about it now was that the look was on a fourteen-year-old boy.

By the time the rest of his family had gotten to them, Ryan had the deer ready to haul out. At first, Flint thought Ryan was just trying to hurry and dress out the deer, but as Ryan hurried more the more, Flint realized that he was hurrying so they could leave. Ryan's wife and kids could see his urgency, especially after getting the buck back to camp. Ryan insisted that everyone break camp the moment they got back. He knew that there was something extremely uneasy about Flint, and he didn't want his family around him anymore. Word of how Flint reacted on the hunt got around town quickly. After that, the community had completely given up on him.

When Flint was sixteen, he began to go hunting on his own. He took all the survival skills that Ryan had taught him and began expanding on them by himself. He spent all his time in the woods. The more he pushed his time to be alone in the woods, the faster he became an outsider of the community. Eventually, everyone just started to see him as the crazy kid. Flint's mother tried everything she could to hold onto hope. She pushed him to be more social and outgoing, but nothing she did helped. The older he got, the more comfortable Flint became with being an outcast.

Five o'clock hit, and Flint headed right home. He drove an old rust-covered pickup truck that rattled as he drove. Flint was never a person to put care into his personal possessions. When he arrived home, all his hunting gear was sitting in the corner of the living room. He had been preparing his gear for a few days now and started to go over it again double and triple checking everything even though he knew it was ready. Regard less, he had to be sure he was ready for the hunt. He headed to bed around eight o'clock, prepared to wake up early to head for the mountains. Tossing and turning, Flint's excitement wouldn't let him fall asleep. This is the time of the year he lives for. By three a.m., Flint found himself lying on his back staring up at the ceiling, waiting for his alarm to go off.

Beep, beep, beep.

Shooting out of bed like a rocket, Flint dressed quickly and threw his old military surplus backpack into the bed of the truck; everything he would need was either strapped to it or inside of it. Going back to the house, he grabbed his rifle. The rifle was old, the bluing had started to wear off, and the wooden stock was in desperate need of a new coat of finish. *All the same, it's just fine the way it is*, he thought. It was his father's old rifle, and as far as Flint was concerned, it was the only thing of value that he had left of the man.

With all his gear loaded, Flint started up the old truck. As the truck sat idling, warming the engine, he began to think about the day before. It had reminded him of all the people that had talked behind his back throughout his life. His blood began to boil. *I wasn't the one with the problems, it has always been them. I don't need anyone.* He shifted the truck into gear and began to drive to the gas station, one last stop to top off with fuel before heading out of town. Flint couldn't shake the thoughts of his past as he pulled up to the gas pumps. Anger and bitterness filled him. Everyone he had ever known had either given up on him or had been happy to walk out of his life. Everyone in his life had only pretend to care about him, just like Ryan and his family. Even his own mother. They had tolerated him for a while, but never really cared about him. The only time he was ever happy was when he was alone, hunting something. The only true enjoyment he ever felt was watching the light fade out of something's eyes.

With a full tank of gas, Flint was ready to go. Pulling out on to the road, he turned the truck to leave town and head toward the mountains. His mind continued to race the farther he traveled out of town. He was the only vehicle on the road, but he knew once he got to the mountains that he would see all the other camps until he parked and began to hike farther into the back country. Even then, he would run into one or two people.

Flint couldn't wait to get a chance at his game, though. He was really hoping to have a challenging hunt this season. Sometimes hunting deer wasn't much of a challenge anymore. He loved the feeling he got when he killed something. It gave him the ultimate feeling of power and control. That's when he got a strange thought. The truck started to fade off into the darkness. *What if this time I didn't come back? What if I just stayed out there?* Flint thought to himself.

Chapter 2

Twenty Years Later

The crack of rifle shot broke the air, followed by the quick ping of a metal target. Then another shot broke the air. This time, though, there was no ping after. A man lifted his head from the rifle scope, turning to the man next to him. "You know, Ethan, if you spent more than just a weekend or two before the hunt shooting, you might hit a target once in your life."

Ethan continued looking through the scope of his rifle. He worked the bolt and fired off another round. *Ping.* Slowly, Ethan took his hand off the trigger raising it to a ninety-degree angel. He turned his head, his long beard pushing against the stock of the rifle as he slowly raised his middle finger. "Vin, I miss one shot every once in a while, and you refuse to ever shut the hell up. "Ethan said as a giant smirk rolled across his face.

"If I didn't give you shit, who else would?" Vin asked.

"Oh, you give me plenty of shit now, but on a day when I outshoot you, heaven forbid I give you shit." Ethan said waving his hands around.

The range master blew the whistle signaling the end of the shooting session. "Cease fire! Go ahead and head down range to check your target." The range master said. Vin and Ethan both stood up, grabbing a new target each and heading down range. "Alright, let's end this for now being as we both have brand new rifles," Vin said as he stapled up his target.

Ethan finished placing his target and turned. "So, we're going to have a little competition?" Ethan asked.

"Oh, that's for damn sure," Vin said.

They both get back to their benches and settled down. Vin took his hat off, running his hand through his shoulder length hair. As he placed his hat back on his head, Vin ran his other hand through his short-cut beard. "Okay, here's what I'm thinking. We each have a five-round magazine. We each put one in the pipe, then load up one mag. Six shots. Two three-shot groups." Vin reached into his pocket and pulled out a quarter. "Both groupings have to be inside the edges of the quarter."

Ethan let out a slight laugh, "Alright, alright. What are we playing for then?"

Vin paused, thinking for a second. "Okay, winner gets first call on an elk when we get up to the mountain."

"Well hell, then for damn sure I'm in. Get ready, cause it's not even going to be close," Ethan replied.

The range master blew his whistle, "Range is hot!"

Vin and Ethan both loaded their magazines, placing one round in the chamber before inserting them. "Game on," Vin shouted. A shot cracked from Ethan's rifle, closely followed by one from Vin's. Working the bolts on their guns, they both sent out two more rapid fire shots.

Ethan lifted his head and turned to Vin. "Shit, that is going to be close."

They both adjusted to aim at a new spot on their targets. Vin shot first. This time a few seconds went by before Ethan's rifle fired. Vin's second shot rang out just after Ethan's first. Ethan fired his second shot as Vin fired his third.

Having fired all six of his rounds, Vin peered through his scope. It was a hundred yards down range to look at his groups. "Oh yeah, those two groups are going to be damn hard to beat," he said as he turned to look over Ethan's target. The five shots were just as close as Vin's. "This is going to come right down to the wire," Vin said in a mock sports announcer voice, "one shot left. Is he going to bring it home, or is he going to choke?" Ethan fired his rifle.

"Oh, hell yeah! Couldn't hold it together under pressure. Now raise my hand! Come on raise my hand!" Vin shouted as he stood up.

Begrudgingly, Ethan stood up and grabbed Vin's hand, raising it in victory. "Remember, we all pull a shot once in a while," Ethan said.

Vin and Ethan both began to pack their rifles back into their cases. "I'm glad to see you got your gun back in time for the hunt," Vin said, relinquishing his taunt over his win.

"Yeah, I was a little late getting on the list at the custom shop. If not, I would have had to pull out one of my older rifles," Ethan replied. "After our last two hunts, I think these changes are really going to help us out."

"Dude, the way we had the guns set up when we were in Africa, we might as well have thrown the scopes in the trash." Vin said.

The range master walked up to Vin and Ethan, "Hey, you don't see many guys packing scout rifles nowadays. Putting open sights and scopes on a bolt gun is going away in a hurry. Plus, you two are normally packing some new and improved long-range set of rifles," he said.

"We had a few of our last trips where things ended up being close-range rather than the normal circumstances, so we thought we would change things up," Vin said.

Ethan's phone rang.

Vin turned his head as Ethan pulled it out of his pocket and saw the screen. "Ashley? She called you like an hour and a half ago," Vin said.

"Just calm down, this is the first hunting season she's going through," Ethan retorted as he answered the phone and turned to walk away from the range.

Vin turned back to the range master, "He should have known better then to start dating a city girl."

The range master laughed, "He's got a long road to go on that one."

Vin turned to see that Ethan was still on the phone. Shaking his head, Vin picked up both gun cases and began to walk to his truck. Reaching the back of his truck, Vin set both rifles down to lower the tailgate, then placed them into the bed of the truck. Vin noticed Ethan approaching as he closed the tailgate.

"Sounds good, I'll see you in a while. Bye." Ethan wasn't watching as he walked up to the back of the truck and proceeded to smack his shin into Vin's trailer hitch. "Ah, damn it, that hurts," Ethan yelled out. He groaned a little bit and lifted his hat, running his hand underneath it along his shaved head, down his face, and through his beard.

"That was sure smart," Vin said sarcastically.

"You know, eight years later my shin is still sensitive as hell," Ethan said.

"Do I need to go get you a tampon?"

Ethan looked up at Vin with his hat slightly tilted off his head and smirked as he flipped Vin off.

Vin leaned on the side of the truck bed. "Okay, dude, what was this one about?" Vin asked.

"She was just calling to check in this time," Ethan answered with a roll of his eyes.

"Look, dude, she's a hell of a gal, but you have to get her to calm down. She is going to go insane when we leave cell service. Assuming you don't. I mean, this summer she about died when we did the scouting trips, a full hunting trip might push here over the edge." Vin said.

"I know, I know. When we get over to your place tonight, can you get Kasey to help me out a bit? I think another woman will help out a lot," Ethan said.

Flashing Ethan a thumbs-up, Vin walked around and climbed into the driver's seat of the truck, inserted the key, and turned over the motor.

Ethan walked around to the passenger side, but before he reached the door he bent down and rubbed his shin. His leg was still stinging with pain. He pulled up the pant leg, exposing the skin. The area from just below his knee to his ankle was covered in scars. He rubbed the front of his leg, then lowered his pant leg and opened the door to the truck. Because he was so short — maybe five-foot-nine — Ethan had to reach up and grab the handle to pull himself in.

"Hey, if you would grow up, you could just step into the truck," Vin said.

"Oh, just because someone is over six foot, he's got all sorts of jokes," Ethan replied with a laugh.

"Well, let's get the hell out of here. I think the rifles are ready for the hunt," Ethan said

"Yeah, then I can help Kasey get things started for dinner before you and Ashley show up," Vin replied as he shifted the truck into drive.

Chapter 3

The Night Before

Ethan stepped out of Vin's truck, grabbing his shooting bag and rifle from the back as Vin rolled the window down.

"Alright, you two are still swinging over later, right?" Vin asked.

"Yup, Ashley and I will be over around seven," Ethan replied.

Vin shot Ethan a thumbs-up and drove off.

Ethan rented the first house you see upon driving into their small town. It was all by itself, right on the corner of the local farmer's field. He had rented it after the farmer's mother had passed on. It was quite the little farmhouse that the farmer's mother had kept almost perfectly stuck in time. It was what all his friends called a 1940s old lady's dream house, which thought always made Ethan laugh when entering the home.

Ethan walked through the front door, heading straight to the office. The room had flower wallpaper and light blue carpet. His gun safe sat against one wall next a closet with all his hunting clothes. Against the wall opposite the safe was a bench for reloading ammunition and, sitting next to the safe, was his hunting equipment, packed for the upcoming trip. As Ethan moved the rifle case next to the backpack, the doorbell rang.

"Hey, you're hear an hour early," Ethan said.

Ashley walked through the door, "Well, since you guys are leaving in the morning, I thought I would try to spend a little extra time with you," she said.

"Let me just get changed," Ethan turned down the hall, heading for the bedroom while Ashley walked past and into the living room. Even from the bedroom Ethan could hear her soft laugh. "Oh hell, what are you laughing about now?" Ethan asked.

"You know what it is," Ashley replied.

Ethan walked around the corner to the living room carrying his socks in one hand and his shoes in the other. "You're going to be laughing at this room forever, aren't you?" Ethan asked.

"I mean, it's just hilarious to look at. You live in this picture perfect little old lady's house and the décor is all the animals from your hunting trips. It just makes me laugh every time I see it," Ashley said.

Ethan sat on the couch to put his shoes on while laughing and shaking his head, "Well, when I get a house built, I'll design it a bit differently," Ethan said, leaning back and sinking into the couch as Ashley sat down next to him.

Vin had just excited his truck and began to walk into his house with his rifle case and range bag. He lived some distance outside of town, having purchased a few acres on a hill overlooking a river bend. It was a log cabin style home and the only house around for about two miles. Basically, it was his dream house. Once inside, Vin headed right to his office. It was set up just like Ethan's, and he set his rifle right next to his already prepared hunting gear. Then he took the range bag over to a closet and began putting everything away.

"You guys weren't in too big of a hurry to get back."

Vin heard the comment, smiled, and closed the closet door to look and see his wife, Kasey, standing in the doorway. "You know better than to hold me to the time I tell you, "Vin laughed.

Kasey rolled her eyes, turning to walk away while shaking her head. "Well, either way, you need to get the BBQ going before Ethan and Ashley get here," Kasey said over her shoulder.

Vin headed for the kitchen and grabbed a few steaks and ribs that he had been defrosting, setting them on a plate on the kitchen counter. Next, he walked out the back door to the cookout area he had built. He had spent an entire summer laying the brick around the circular fire pit, building the wooden table for everyone to eat on, and crafting the wooden skeleton frame around the entire thing. The frame had three wooden pillars holding it up, but the fourth was a stone pillar with a cut out in the middle and a hollow chimney going all the way up and out the top. He had even built moveable cooking racks into the cutout.

Vin headed right for a bag of charcoal and began to pour it into his homemade grill. He lit the charcoal and walked back into the house to get the meat. After placing it on the grill, he set the four chairs around the fire pit and began to build a fire. Once he got the logs lit, Vin walked back into the kitchen. Kasey was preparing a few sides to go with the meat. He kissed her on the cheek, grabbed a pair of tongs and a spatula, and began heading back outside when the doorbell rang.

"Hey, can you get that? My hands are full at the moment," Kasey said.

Vin turned around, shooting her a thumbs-up, then went to get the door. "Hey! You guys are a little early," Vin said opening the front door.

"Well, what the hell else were we going to do? We just figured we would come over and help you guys set things up," Ethan replied. Ethan and Ashley followed Vin inside, both carrying the drinks for the evening. Ashley set a few down on the kitchen counter, then Vin took them and placed them in the Fridge.

"It's so good to see you!" Ashley squealed as she ran over to Kasey, giving her a huge hug.

"Well, you two have fun in here. We will go check on the other food," Vin said. He and Ethan both headed out the back door. Vin went right to the grill, flipping the steaks and checking on the ribs. By now, the fire in the pit was burning extremely hot and he could feel the heat on the entire patio. "Hey, can you grab the one cover over there and unroll it?" Vin asked Ethan. There were three covers over the skeleton frame that they could unroll to block the sun or keep the heat in. They both unrolled one on each side and left the area over the fire pit in the middle open. After about twenty minutes, Vin called to the women in the house, "Hey, the meat is done, head on out here."

The couples sat down and ate dinner together. Afterward, they got a few more drinks and some supplies to make s'mores and settled down around the fire. It was an overcast night, and the darkness had settled all around them. They had all the outside lights shut off on the house. The only thing that broke the darkness of the night was the fire. "I love the feeling of sitting around a fire. It's the most comforting feeling you can have," Vin said.

"I'll tell you what, since the first time you took me up into the mountains for a fishing trip, once that darkness settles in around you it can get so creepy," Kasey said.

"How far in the middle of the mountains were you guys?" Ashley asked.

"Oh, when either one of them plans a trip hunting, fishing, or even hiking they are never anywhere near civilization," Kasey answered.

"Yeah, but you are never quite about having me get a fire going as fast as I can," Vin interjected.

"Well of course. I don't care how many flashlights or lanterns I have, nothing can comfort me like a campfire," Ashley said. "

"Right now, the fire is nice, but with the complete darkness around me, I can't help but think about what could be out in the darkness watching us," Ashley said as a cold shiver ran down her spine.

"We get that feeling quite often, but you have to understand what Kasey meant. That creeping feeling you get is when you look out into the darkness around us right?" Vin asked Ashley.

"Well, yes," Ashley answered.

"It's that same feeling you get when your alone in your house and the power goes out. You aren't afraid because you are alone in the dark, you're afraid that you're not alone, correct?" Vin asked.

"Oh yeah, that's it. You hit the nail on the head," Ashley said.

"Now, you say being around the fire is nice, but imagine if we didn't have the fire burning right now," Vin said.

"I'm not going to lie, even here right next to your house that would still freak me out. If we were out in the middle of the mountains or the desert, I would have a straight up horror movie playing in my head," Ashley replied.

"Normally, people imagine the worst-case scenario anyways, so it wouldn't be much different," Ethan quickly interjected with a laugh.

"Oh, quite you," Ashley shot back.

"Anyways, the point I'm trying to make here is that the fire is the light at the end of the tunnel. It's that ultimate comforting feeling that helps you get through the night. Not only does it bring you the light with the ability to see your surroundings, but do you feel that warmth on your face? That's the other thing it brings you, the good light and that nice warm comfort that gets you through the night. It's always warmer with a fire, and it gives you that very protective feeling that you need," Vin said.

"I'm not so sure about that," Ashley said. "Now, I'm kind of new to this living in the country thing, and the fire is nice, but it's what is out in that darkness that gives me the creeps."

"Oh, you will get used to it. We will get you used to living out in the middle of nowhere before too long," Ethan said.

Kacey was laughing under her breath as she put another marshmallow onto a stick.

"Now what has you laughing over there?" Vin asked.

"Well, I grew up in a small town as well, but I'm still not used to all the crap you two guys always get yourselves into," Kasey said.

Ashley's eyes went wide as saucers as she slowly turned her head towards Ethan.

"Now what is this look all about?" Ethan asked, chuckling.

"Are there some stories that I should know about?" Ashley shook her head, "Oh, wait why am I asking you? You will just give me the same answer as always."

"And what answer is it that I always give?" Ethan asked.

"That it was blown way out of proportion, and I just need to calm down. So, this time let's ask someone else." Raising her eyebrows Ashley turned her head to look at Kasey. "So, what are some of these troubles they have gotten into?" Ashley asked.

"Where do I start?" Kasey laughed. "I have been around for a whole bunch and have heard about countless adventures they have had dating back to at least high school. The most recent one I can think of would have to be that coyote hunting trip they went on last year. That one got a little out of hand," Kasey said.

"Well, who would like to start telling the tale?" Ashley asked.

Both men smirked and ducked their heads whiles continuing to cook their marshmallows.

"Well, it looks like you have the bigger smirk on your face, Vin, so you need to get talking," Ashley said.

"Okay, okay. We had tried to sneak down south for this quick weekend trip, wanting to get one more trip in before the winter set in," Vin said. "

"I'm feeling that there is a kicker to this story coming up," Ashley said.

"We always try to be prepared for all things that could happen, but although we did a weather check, it was late November, and the weather can change on a dime. We had been in the mountains for two days and got a little greedy. We had found a honey hole; there were coyotes everywhere. So, we decided to stay for an extra day. We brought our hot tents to sleep in, which are backpacking tipi style tents you can put stoves in to stay warm, because it had gotten cold already." Ethan said.

"Then we woke up to complete snow cover," Vin finished.

"Ashley closed her eyes, let out a sigh, and lowered her head. "So how did you two get out of this one?" she asked.

"It got a little touch and go making it out of the mountains, but everything was just fine," Vin laughed.

"So, between all these stupid adventures you two go on and that messed up set of scars on your shin, I can't believe all the crap you guys still get into," Ashley said.

"You know, I have always wanted to know how you got those scars," Kasey said.

"Yeah, when we were kids there was a family in town that had a really mean Rottweiler named Crowbar. I was riding by that house one day on my bike and the dog had gotten out of the backyard and came after me, running me down," Ethan said.

"Jeez, I had no idea. How old were you?" Kasey asked.

"Around eleven or twelve," Ethan answered.

Kasey and Ashley both stood up to go and get some more drinks. While their backs were turned, Ethan turned to Vin, shooting him a look. Vin looked completely surprised.

Kasey and Ashley both returned, the couples spent a few more hours trading stories and laughs before deciding to call it a night. Ethan and Ashley headed for her car as Vin and Kasey followed them to the front of the house. Ashley gave Kasey a hug as Vin patted Ethan on the back. "Alright, be ready. I will be at your house to pick you up just a little after eleven," He said.

"Sounds good, bud. I will be waiting by ten-thirty," Ethan replied.

After Ethan and Ashley had left, Vin began to bring in a few things from the tables outside. They had used paper plates, so there wasn't a whole lot to clean up. After moving what they needed to inside, Kasey placed the few dishes that needed a wash into the dishwasher. "Hey, do you need a hand in there?" Vin asked.

"No, just go make sure all of your things are ready for the morning. I don't want to see you rushing around at the last minute or rushing to the store trying to find things that you have forgotten," Ashley said.

"Jeez, you act like I may have done that a time or two before."

"No, never. You always have all your gear extremely organized," Kasey replied sarcastically. They both chuckled as Vin walked into the office to where he had set his gear from earlier that day.

Vin went to his backpack right away. It was already packed, but he started to pull things out to make sure it was packed just how he wanted it. First, he checked all the things he had hanging from the outside of the back. Next, he checked the tripod that was strapped to the side. Then he moved to a side zip pocket that held the spotting scope that attached to the tripod; it would allow them to spot animals at extremely long ranges and decide how to proceed with a hunt on what they could find. He also checked for all his water purification equipment and first aid gear. Next were fire starter, knives, and rope, followed by some cooking equipment and the other clothes he would need. He had his tipi tent, sleeping bag equipment, and a day pack strapped to the outside. The backpack also had a gun scabbard, but he wouldn't use that yet.

Then he walked over to the closet and pulled out a soft gun

case. He set it on the floor then went to pull his rifle from the other case from earlier in the day. Opening the case to move the rifle over, he heard a comment from behind him.

"A brand-new gun. You guys would have a million dollars if you didn't spend it on all your damn hunting gear," Kasey said from the entryway.

"What are you talking about?" Vin asked with a laugh.

"You guys get new guns, get nice backpacks. Oh, and every time I turned around you are buying more camo from Kryptek," Kasey said.

Vin turned around and stood up waving his hands, "Hey now, you need to settle down. One, when I buy hunting gear, I make sure I buy good reliable gear. Now I'm not positive, but haven't I caught you wearing my Kryptek quite often?" Vin said.

"That's not the point," Kasey replied.

"Second, just remember, when I die be sure to sell all of my stuff for what it's actually worth, not what I told you I bought it for," Vin said with a big smile on his face.

Kasey rolled her eyes and began shaking her head as she turned and walked out of the room.

Chapter 4

Preparing to Leave

The following morning, Vin was awake bright and early even though he wasn't picking up Ethan until eleven. By the time Kasey woke up, Vin had already loaded his truck and was cooking some breakfast. Grateful that breakfast almost ready for her, Kasey quickly got ready for work so they could eat together. "So, you two are leaving today to head to the mountains. Friday, you guys will spend hiking to where you're hunting. Then Saturday, the season starts right?" Kasey asked.

"Yes. Then we have plans to hunt until the following Saturday, unless we both get an Elk before then," Vin replied.

"If next Saturday is the last day of the hunt, when is the time I need to call search and rescue if you haven't checked in by?" Kasey asked.

"Give us until Sunday night at six, any later than that means something has gone wrong. How does that sound?"

"That works for me. Be safe, have fun, and I will see you when you get back. I love you," Kasey said.

"I'm always safe," Vin quickly replied.

"Sure, you are," Kasey shot back as she gave him a quick kiss and headed for the door to leave.

"I promise, I will be safe and love you too," Vin replied as she walked out the front door. Vin walked around the house making sure he hadn't forgotten anything, and double checked that he had all the emergency supplies as well. He had just a few minutes before he had to leave to go pick up Ethan, so he took a quick stroll upstairs, into his man cave. It was an attic style room, and there were things all over the walls from all the adventures that he had taken over the years. There were mini statues from a cruise he and Kasey had taken to Mexico and a few things from their vacation to Ireland, but most of the memorabilia had come from hunting trips and adventures into the mountains. He could look around the room and almost see his entire life through one trip at a time.

He kept the photos of his first adventure right next to the door. He and Ethan had gone on this trip together. They had both been twelve years old at the time. Their fathers had been hunting buddies as well, and it was the first trip their dads had taken them on. It was one of his favorite photos from the old days. Both he and Ethan had huge smiles while standing next to their dads and the massive deer they had shot that year. All it had taken was that first trip and both boys had been hooked right away.

The next few years they were able to start buying permits so they could try and get themselves a deer. For both boys, the experience of hunting with their dads was unlike anything else. They loved the adventure and the time spent with their dads. They just couldn't get enough of it.

A little farther down the wall hung a photo that was taken when he and Ethan were sixteen years old, it was of the first deer each of them got on their own without their dads. From the time they were each fourteen, they had been encouraged to have some sort of job. They normally worked at the local supermarket, but the summer they had turned sixteen they both got a second job working for one of the local farmers. They weren't making much for pay from him because they had worked it out so that if they worked for him all summer, once they fall hit, they would be the only ones allowed to hunt on his land.
That was the first time that Vin and Ethan went hunting on their own. They spent the season tracking deer in the river bottoms. They were very patient and took their time and, towards the last days of the season, they had both gotten themselves a nice buck.

Vin began to look up and down the walls, seeing the photos and thinking of all the fun and crazy adventures they had been involved in. He and Ethan had both gotten jobs right out of high school so they could start making money for all the places they wanted to go hunting. There were deer, elk, pronghorn, black bear, and a caribou all from North America mounted on the walls. There were photos from dove hunting in Argentina and their recent big adventure to Namibia; checking that one off the bucket list was one of the craziest things they had ever done.

There was a photo of both Vin, Ethan, and their hunting guide, Super, standing around a downed hippo. Staring at the photo made Vin twitch a little. Neither one of them had been there to shoot a hippo. They had traveled to their hunting area by boat and had been hustling to try and get back to it despite the dangers of the river, not wanting to be on the water after dark. Vin remembered that as they had returned to the boat, all three men walking toward the bank with guns at the ready, there was a flash of movement as a hippo burst through the glass-like surface of the water and charged onto the bank.

Vin and Ethan both fired a round from their rifles. With the small caliber of the guns, the shots didn't even slow down the hippo. From behind them, Super drew down on the animal with his massive, dangerous game double rifle. The concussion of the rifle was earth shaking. Super was the best shot they had ever seen, and the bullet struck the hippo right between the eyes. It fell, dead, at Vin and Ethan's feet.

Even though it had been a moment where both men had come seconds away from death and thinking about it made Vin's blood run cold, he couldn't wait to go back. It was an adventure that was checked off his bucket list and was immediately written back on.

Looking around the room, there was one photo that always caught his eye, and not for a good reason. Even with what had happened in Africa, this photo overpowered every terrifying experience he had ever had. They had been twenty-one, attempting to bring down a mule deer in Wyoming. Thinking about that trip sent a cold chill down Vin's spine. He immediately shook it off, walked out of the room, locked the door to his house, and got in his truck to go pick up Ethan.

Ethan just finished setting all his gear next to the front door. He looked down at his watch, seeing that he still had roughly twenty-five minutes until Vin would be there, and headed back into his office to close his gun safe. He didn't just use it to lock up guns, he also kept all his valuables in it. He looked the safe up and down, making sure everything was in it. He smiled, catching sight of a small black box at the front of one of the shelves. *I will make sure to figure out the perfect time to give that to Ashley when I get back. I don't want her to get too excited while I'm gone*, Ethan thought to himself. With a giant smile on his face, Ethan closed the safe door, locking it.

He then started to walk through the house, making sure that everything had been shutoff and the doors were all locked. Once

Ethan had checked everything, he walked into the living room. He looked around the room as he sat down to watch TV for a few minutes and one photo on the wall caught his attention. It was the one from his and Vin's Wyoming mule deer hunt, showing both hiking through the mountains. There were no trophies from that hunt on either of their walls—there were only two things that they had kept as mementos from that trip into the mountains.

Ethan brought his attention to the TV, absentmindedly rubbing his hand on his shin. He shrugged the memories of that trip away, lightly shaking his head. Just as he leaned back to get comfortable, his doorbell rang. Ethan looked down at his watch, *Vin's early*, he thought. Shrugging it off, he opened the door. His eyes widened and his head tilted back. He was completely shocked to find Ashley standing there.

"Um, aren't you supposed to be at work? Why didn't you just use your key and walk in?" Ethan asked

"I took the morning off because I wanted to make sure I got to see you before you guys headed out. I thought that it would help me feel better about things, and I wouldn't worry so much. And I didn't just walk in because its mid-day and I was worried you might think it was someone breaking in," Ashley said.

Ethan tilted his head and began to laugh, "Yeah that was probably a good call," He said.

"Well, you have all of your gear? You didn't forget anything?" Ashley asked.

Ethan ran his hand through his beard as he began to think. "Shit! I did, hold on," Ethan said, running into the other room. He quickly returned, holding a small bottle of 10th Mountain Rye Whiskey and a Milky Way candy bar.

"Um, that's what you forgot?" Ashley asked confused.

"Okay this will take some explaining. So, as we were joking last night, occasionally things get a little touch and go. Well, Vin and I each carry a bottle and a candy bar in our packs. The bottles are like six years old. We've never opened them, but it's just a little joke that one day we're going to be in a bad spot and we'll each take one last shot then enjoy our last candy bar," Ethan explained.

"Oh boy, that is comforting," Ashley said, rolling her eyes.

There was a loud honk from outside. Ethan peeked out the window, seeing Vin's truck pull up to the house. "Alright, babe, do you mind helping be haul this stuff to the truck?" Ethan asked.

"Yup, no problem," Ashley replied, grabbing the backpack, and throwing it on her back. "Good hell this thing is heavy," she gasped.

Ethan let out a laugh while picking up the rifle case, "Well, I mean I will be living out of that backpack for a while, so it would make sense that is quite heavy," Ethan replied. Trying not to sound sarcastic.

Ashley headed toward Vin's truck as Ethan locked the house behind them, setting the pack down next to the back tire and letting out a huge sigh of relief.

Ethan walked up to the truck. He tossed the backpack into the bed and slid the gun into the back seat. "Alright, babe, we are out of here," Ethan said.

"You guys promise to be safe?" Ashley asked with a slight tremble in her voice.

"Yes, of course we do. The goal is always to keep out of trouble," Ethan replied.

"I know, but being as this is my first time dealing with a hunting season, I'm kind of freaking out a little bit. Anything could happen, and I don't want you to end up breaking a bone or something and then getting suck out there and getting killed."

"That's fair," Ethan said. "I'll tell you what, there is a little mom-and-pop gas station at the base of the mountains that we will hit toward the end of the trip in. I will have enough cell service of to make a quick call and let you know we made it that far," Ethan said.

"Well, it won't calm me down completely, but it will help," Ashley replied.

"Everything will be fine, but if you get nervous or anything, just give Kasey a call. She has been through this many times and will help you out," Vin interjected.

Ethan gave Ashley a hug followed by a kiss, then opened the door and climbed in as Vin turned over the motor. "Try not to worry about a thing. Just wait, after a couple of trips you'll be telling me to hurry the hell up and get out of the house," Ethan said with a laugh. Ashley looked back at him slightly confused but smiling. "I will call you in a while to check in," Ethan said as Vin shifted the truck into reverse and began to pull away from the house.

Vin chuckled as they began to head out of town. Ethan slowly turned his head toward his friend. "Would you care to share with the class?" Ethan asked.

"Well, I was just thinking you got yourself quite the stage one clinger there, buddy," Vin answered.

"Me? I have a stage one clinger? Um, I remember many times, and I mean a freaking shit ton of times, where Kasey, who now basically boots your ass out the door, had complete meltdowns that you had gone missing or one of us had been killed or hurt because we hadn't checked in at least once every twenty-four hours," Ethan said.

"Oh, come on, Kasey was never that bad," Vin laughed.

"Not that bad? Have you completely forgotten about that black bear hunt we went on the second year the two of you were together?" Ethan asked.

"That was a completely different circumstance," Vin answered.

"We don't know that yet," Ethan replied.

"On that black bear hunt, we got a little carried away. We were two days late getting back, she kind of had a right to be freaking out," Vin said.

"Yeah, and if you hadn't called her when you did, she would have called search and rescue," Ethan said.

"Like I said, it was a different circumstance."

"Hasn't she also been hounding you to by some sort of GPS or satellite phone for, oh I don't know, a year or two now? What happened to that?" Ethan asked with a laugh.

"Hey now. Okay, she has her little freak outs too here and there. Also, I'm still working on getting the phone, so calm down," Vin jokingly answered.

"Oh, sure you are," Ethan answered sarcastically.

Chapter 5

The Last of Civilization

Six hours later, the men had reached the small town just outside of where they would be hunting. This town had one paved road as the main street and probably close to ten houses. They pulled into the gas station that also acted as the post office. The sign on the side of the building read Pop Store. The station has just two gas pumps. As Vin put the truck in park, he saw the clock read quarter to five in the afternoon. At this time in the day, there was only one old Chevy truck that belonged to the couple who owned the store parked around back. Vin and Ethan had gotten to know the store and its owners well as they had stopped in many times throughout their scouting trips during the summer. Vin stepped out and began to fuel up the truck while Ethan walked around the back of the store to make his phone call to Ashley. Looking up over the bed of the truck, Vin could see Ethan walking away, *Shit, I'm sure glad Kasey has at least calmed down past that stage,* he thought.

Vin reached into the cab and grabbed a light jacket while the truck filled with fuel. Standing by the gas pumps, Vin could see how late it was getting. The store rested in the shadow of the mountain, and Vin stared at the top of the peaks, feeling a slight chill from the wind on his neck. He grinned. *I don't know why, but I feel like this is going to be one of the craziest trips we've ever had,* Vin thought to himself.

The fuel pump clicked, and Vin put it on its stand, put the cap back on the tank, and headed inside to pay. He took a quick peak around the back of the store and could see Ethan talking on the phone. "Hey, get in here and we'll grab something to take with to eat tonight,"

Vin yelled. Ethan turned around and held up one finger, signaling for Vin to hold on for a minute. Just then, Vin heard his cell phone go off with an alert message. Pulling it out of his pocket, he saw the front said one new email. He opened the email and read: *Your package has shipped* was the subject. *Shit that was supposed to ship a week ago. I order a damn satellite phone, and it's going to get to my house in the middle of the trip I wanted it for. Now, when it gets to the house, Kasey is going to have a lecture for me when I get back.*

Vin turned around, walking toward the front door to the store. As he reached to open the door, he noticed a sign taped to the inside of the glass. There was a picture of a man close to same age as Vin and Ethan, and right across the top of the poster the words: Missing, any information would help. Vin's heart sank. That same poster had been there for the last few months; this man had gone missing in the middle of the summer. The report of the man's last location was at the campgrounds at the base of the mountains. The story had been all over the news for a few weeks, but now all that remained were the posters hanging around. The search had been called off three weeks ago. Though the news had treated it like it was just another person that had gone missing in the woods, Vin and Ethan had treated it differently.

No one had found any trace of the man after he left the campground. The thing that he and Ethan had thought was strange was that this man was a very experienced outdoorsman; everything that was put on the news said he had grown up camping, fishing, and hunting very regularly. His family had also reported that these mountains were one of his favorite fishing spots.

Vin continued to stare at the poster for a few more seconds. "I really wonder what could have happened to you," Vin muttered to himself about the man on the poster before pulling the door open and walking into the store.

He looked over, seeing the man standing behind the counter. "Well, how the hell are you, Jed?" Vin said.

"Just same old, same old," Jed replied.

Vin laughed, walked to the back to grab a drink, and then headed back up to the front where they kept fried chicken.

"Well, what will you have?" Jed asked.

"Just give me four pieces, this will be dinner tonight before we head into hunt on foot in the morning."

The door opened, and Ethan walked in.

"Hey, go get a drink. Do you want any of this stuff?" Vin said, pointing to the chicken.

"Yeah, grab me four pieces."

They both walked up to the counter to pay for everything. "I hope you boys have plenty of warm clothes. It looks like rain, and there is a chance of snow in the next few days," Jed said.

"Oh, don't worry. With the amount of money he spends on his camo, he better be kept warm," Ethan said sarcastically.

"Well, maybe one day you will realize how nice my stuff is compared to your army surplus gear," Vin replied. They both thanked the man and began to walk out of the store. Just about halfway to the door, Vin stopped and turned back to the old man. "Hey, have they heard any word on the guy that went missing?" Vin asked.

"Officially, the search has been called off for a few weeks now," Jed replied.

"Officially?"

"Well, the search teams just ruled him as missing and the incident as another accident in the woods, but not everyone around here is convinced that, that is the case," Jed said.

"Alright, you can't just stop the story there now that you have our attention. It sounds like a lot of people think something happened to this guy," Ethan interjected.

"Yeah, well the crazy thing is that no one could find any trace of him. The search teams went up to the lake that he was supposed to be camping by, but nothing was there, not even a candy bar wrapper or a sign of a fire. It's almost like he just up and disappeared. They found his truck at the campgrounds, but that was it. No note in it or anything. His family has come up here as much as they possibly can. The sheriff, he even goes up and takes a look every now and again, but with no tracks, sign, or anything to give you any idea of where to start, well after a while you're just walking around in the woods, and then how long is it until you get lost up there yourself?" Jed said.

Vin and Ethan looked at each other. The sober look on both their faces showed that they were thinking hard about what they had just heard.

"The reports say that weather could get rough up there this week. You boys make sure to keep your heads on a swivel," Jed said as he waved them both out of the store.

"Well, that sure gives you a warm cuddly feeling, doesn't it?" Vin said.

"True, but you have to remember, dude, creepy weird shit happens in the woods all the time all over the world," Ethan replied.

"I know, I know. But there's normally some sort of sign or indication to what could have happened right?" Vin asked.

"Not always. I can think of a bunch of news stories about people going missing in the woods for as long as I can remember. You know as well as I do that people do stupid shit that gets them caught in trouble all the time. Out of nowhere, people will deviate from their plans which lands them in extreme danger. Sometimes even right to the brink of getting killed. Like in this case, this guy probably decided to change his plans right at the last minute and thought screw it, I'm not going back into cell range to call and tell my family the change in plans. The search teams are probably looking in the wrong place," Ethan said.

"I know that happens all the time, but . . ."

"Remember, we have been there too," Ethan cut him off, leaning on the hood of the truck with both hands.

Vin let a laugh out under his breath, "Oh, I know."

"See, just throw it in the back of your mind, and, like always, we just got to be smart," Ethan said.

As they finished up talking, they both began to get into the truck as another pulled up to the gas pump beside them. It had just come down from the mountains that Vin and Ethan were going to.

It didn't even take the door on the truck to open to hear that the two men were arguing. "Good hell, you're a dumbass," one man said as he opened the door and got out of the truck.

From the other side of the cab, a second man yelled out, "Hey, for the last time, I didn't lose your shit."

"Then we left a bunch of stuff back at the house? Or what, did someone come into camp in the middle of the night and steal it?" The driver replied, slamming his door closed.

"Hey, man, is everything alright?" Vin asked.

The man jammed the fuel pump into the truck before looking up at Vin. "No," he replied, "my idiot brother over there lost a bunch of our gear and food and now is claiming he has no idea what happened to it."

"What all is missing?" Vin asked.

"Well, we got back to our camp and I went to get our food out of the truck, but only about a third of our food was there, so obviously someone didn't remember to put it in the truck. Also, I bought myself a brand-new pair of binoculars last week for hunting season. He was screwing around with them on the way up, but now they are nowhere to be found," the man said.

"That sucks, man. We are just heading up to get our camp site up ourselves," Vin replied.

"What area are you guys heading up to?"

"Well, we have some serious hiking to do tomorrow. We are going to set up our camp by Cliff Lake," Vin answered.

"Oh hell, you guys are really going to get back there. I don't know of anyone that has even headed back in that far before. I was going to asked if you would keep an eye out for me, but you guys won't even be close to where we were. We were on the same side of the range, but we were way below where you guys will be," he said.

"Look out for what?" Vin asked.

"My grandpa gave me his old revolver a few years back. It's an old thirties period gun. I normally carry it while I'm hunting, just as a quick backup in case I need it. Anyways, it seems to have gone missing as well." As he said it, the man pointed to the cab of the truck as if to blame his brother. "I was going to ask you to keep an eye out for it, but we were way below you guys. We were on the north fork meadows, so there is no way you're going to come across it," he said.

"Well, all I can do is wish you guys luck on getting your gear back in order," Vin said. He and Ethan both got into the truck and left the store. They sat in silence for a few moments before Vin turned to Ethan. "What do you think of that?" he asked.

"What do you mean?" Ethan replied. "Well, that one brother seemed pretty damn sure that he packed all of their gear. Plus, the items can be misplaced, but having forgotten half of your food? Don't you find that pretty strange?" Vin said.

"Yeah, I'm not going to lie that gave me a creepy feeling," Ethan answered.

"Yeah, me too," Vin murmured.

The temperature kept dropping as the truck climbed higher into the mountain range. The road wasn't maintained this far up, there were large rocks the truck had to drive over and low hanging trees that scratched the windshield and roof. Vin cringed with every screech of branches on metal. The tall pine trees cast shadows, causing the sunset to come faster than normal. It was a long slow drive.

They could make out each camp in the dark by the glow of the fire as they passed them. Reaching the end of the road, they pulled off at the lake that was nestled in one of the top points of the range. Vin parked the truck in a clearing next to the lake where two other trucks, both pulling horse trailers, were parked.

"Looks like these guys headed in sometime today," Ethan said.

"Yeah, and I bet they are quite a ways in," Vin replied. Exiting the truck, the two men grabbed their dinners and headed to the edge of the lake. They lit a small fire and began to eat. It was a dead silent night, and the light from the moon made the still waters look like a sheet of glass. A few hours passed as the men ate and sat by the fire, laughing and telling stories of their past and hopeful future adventures. Finally, they poured water on the fire, making sure it was completely out, and headed back to the truck. Getting back in the front seats, they went to sleep. In the morning, their hike into the back country would begin.

Chapter 6

Into the Backcountry

A beep started going off on Vin's watch, jarring him awake. His eyes opened and looked down at his watch. Four thirty a.m. It was still completely black outside of the truck. Turning his head, Ethan still laid there motionless. Raising his right arm, Vin shoved Ethan on his shoulder, pushing him into the door. Ethan woke immediately. "Good hell, dude, sometimes I think it would take a nuclear bomb to wake your ass up," Vin said.

"What the shit, man, I was getting up. I just wanted to take an extra five if I could," Ethan replied.

"Yeah, I have heard that one before. Then you end up sleeping till the sun comes up. Now get your ass up, we're burning daylight," Vin said as he began to open the truck door.

"If I have to hear 'we're burning daylight' every damn morning on this trip, I swear I'm going to kick your ass before it's over," Ethan replied.

"Oh come on, get over it," Vin said as he ducked back into the truck, smacking Ethan in the chest. They both turned to the back seat, pulling their backpacks out and setting them each in the bed of the truck.

Ethan turned, looking at Vin's pack. "Man, I hope that high priced Gucci bag you got there turns out to be worth a damn," he said.

"Really? Are you giving me shit over this? My bag was literally fifty dollars more than your bag was," Vin shot back.

Ethan threw both his hands into the air while Vin unlocked and lowered the tailgate, "Oh, shit, looks like I found the button this morning," he said as he walked back to the front of the truck. Vin and Ethan both retrieved their guns from the backseat and placed them on the tail gate along with the smaller empty day packs. Each one pulled their rifle out of its case and opened the scabbard on the back of their multi day packs. "Good hell, these things are going to get heavy fast. I'm really glad we had these guns made to be extremely light," Ethan said.

"Until we get over that peak, this is going to royally suck," Vin said pointing to the top of the mountains.

They finished up readying their gear by securing their daypacks. "Alright, get your map and your GPS out. We don't want to forget," Ethan said. They both opened the top pouch on the packs and pulled out GPS trackers, a map, and a compass. Unfolding both maps, they double checked the routes they had already drawn to what would be their base camp. "Do you have a heading set on your compass just in case?" Ethan asked.

"Yes, I have everything set on the map and compass, as well as on my GPS. All we have to do is follow our already scouted trail," Vin replied.

"Okay, I'm just making sure. I don't want to have to be finding things in a hurry if shit hits the fan,"

"Oh, calm down. We've been doing shit like this for how long? How often have things gone south?" Vin asked.

"Well, I can sure think of at least one time," Ethan shot back.

Vin rolled his eyes, "Yeah, and what did we do then? We handled our shit and got out of a shitty situation," Vin said.

Ethan started to shake his head, "Just make sure your GPS is set on the trail," Ethan said. They both clipped the GPSs to their belts. Next, they pulled a headlamp out of each of their packs, setting them to the low red light and making sure that they gave off the smallest signal they could. They swung their packs up onto their backs, clipping the buckles around their chests and the packs belts around their waists. Between them, they carried two of everything; they liked to always have backups of all their emergency gear in case one failed.

They still had two and a half, maybe three hours till sunup.

"Alight, let's get moving. We're going to have to hurry to get to Cliff Lake by tonight. I don't know about you, but I don't want to be dragging into camp well after dark," Vin said.

"Come on, we are starting this thing in the dark, why wouldn't we want to end it that way, too?" Ethan replied.

"It's way too early to have to deal with your shit," Vin said sarcastically, shaking his head. Vin stepped forward, heading for the trail head a few hundred yards from the truck. Just a few feet behind him, Ethan kept a perfect pace.

Vin walked past the sign, heading straight into forest, while Ethan briefly stopped, placing his hand on top of it. He looked up at the sky, then down at the sign, quickly reading it to himself. *North Fork Trail*. Turning his head up, Ethan saw that Vin had gotten a small lead on him. He went to take his first step on the trail but paused, turning his head back over his shoulder. He felt a pressure. His pack was heavy, but that's not what it was. It felt like someone was standing over him, pushing his shoulders down with all their might.

"Hey, you going to hurry your ass up?"

Ethan's head whipped back around when he heard Vin call to him. "Sorry, thought I saw something weird," Ethan replied.

"No worries, just next time make sure to say something," Vin said. Vin turned back around and continued up the trail.

As Ethan started up the trail, he turned his head slowly back over his shoulder, getting one more glance at the moon glimmering over the water. He turned forward and journeyed up the trail. An ice-cold chill shot up his spine. He couldn't shake the feeling that they were being watched as they took off into the darkness.

They made their way up the trail deeper and deeper into the forest, beginning their ascent up the mountain to the lake. This trail wouldn't take them to Cliff Lake though, it would take them to Mirror Lake. Once at Mirror Lake, the North Fork Trail would end. There was another trail, Sheep Creek, that started off the side of Mirror lake and would take them up again, between two mountains, and then back down, eventually ending at Cliff Lake. This mountain range was filled with hundreds if not thousands of small lakes from all the streams that ran throughout the range.

They could make out horse tracks in the mud as they made their way up the trail. "Well, obviously they went this way," Vin said.

"Yeah, but I mean, good hell, it looks like these guys brought every horse they could up here with them," Ethan replied.

"I bet they set up camp up by Mirror Lake. With this many horses, they could set up an amazingly comfortable camp there," Vin said.

"They would also have the means to get up to where we're going to be camping," Ethan pointed out.

"True, but there's been no sign of anyone else going in as far as we are. Also, Sheep Creek basically isn't a trail anymore. That thing is rough unless you're paying extremely close attention. You could get lost on it so damn easy," Vin said.

They didn't have the time it would take to hike the better trail though, it would have added two days to their trip. As it was, they still needed to cover ground fast to make their tight schedule. Earlier in their scouting trips, they had examined the maps and the mountains in the area, looking at all possible trail heads and breaks in the range. The goal was to cut the hike to Cliff Lake by at least half. They found the high point on the trail, the closest point to the tree line of the mountains. They both looked down to check each of their GPSs. "Alright, first check point. Time to speed things up," Vin said.

"It'll speed things up in the long run, but for right now, this part will seriously suck. So, I guess we better hurry up and get it over with," Ethan replied. They both looked up the mountain and could see the tree line off in the distance. Before they moved, they could feel the sun begin to break over the peaks of the mountains. The warmth of the light hit the back of their necks. Both men immediately closed their eyes and rolled their heads back. It was the best feeling they'd had in hours.

They turned from hiking along the side of the mountain to hiking straight up the face, moving away from the clear and maintained trail. Now they turned to a heading on the GPS, following a trail they had made for themselves earlier in the season. They were the only two people that knew the trail existed. They had only made two scouting trips going this way before, so unless someone knew what to were looking for, they would have no idea it was there. Vin continued to lead as he stepped away from the path and moved onto their trail, Ethan following right behind him.

Each man slowly began to move up hill and into the trees. It didn't take long for them both to be completely engulfed by the forest, disappearing into the trees. A person could walk right past them and would have never known they were there. The trees had grown so thick in some places that their packs would drag across the trunks as they tried to squeeze between them. "Good hell, dude, think we could have picked a worse spot to make our own trail?" Ethan asked.

"You're probably right, it is a tad bit snug trying to get through all this shit," Vin sarcastically replied. Trying to see between the trees was a constant battle, but Vin continued to push forward as fast as he could, often taking the time to look back at Ethan. It always annoyed him that Ethan was always going slower than him. Every time Vin turned around to look at him, Ethan would look up and shake his head. As for Ethan, seeing Vin get frustrated over him going at a slower pace always made him laugh.

"You know those two things at the bottom of your legs? Their called feet, it is possible to move them faster you know," Vin shouted.

"One of these days, your constant pushing to go as fast as you can is going to cause us a serious wreck," Ethan shot back.

"You just need to learn to go faster. We've never had any issues," Vin said.

"Oh yeah? What about that deer hunt we did outside of Jackson hole, remember that? Or has your memory conveniently forgotten that one?" Ethan asked.

"Shit, I should have known you would bring that one up. I had one slight moment where I didn't see something, and you're never going to let me live it down," Vin replied.

"Slight? You're going to tell me that one was just a slight miss? That forest wasn't even as thick as this, and we walked right in on that buck. It was only twenty yards away when you walked right past it. Luckily, that massive bastard is hanging on my wall," Ethan said laughing.

"You say I walked past it, but you have never taken the time to think that I just decided to pass on him," Vin replied.

"Hell, every time you don't see something or have a lapse in judgment, I have to hear that you decided to pass or weren't interested. Come on, just own it, you weren't paying attention." Ethan said.

Vin crested to the top of a flat first. "Crap!"

"What we got?" Ethan asked. His lungs were starting to burn, and the weight of the backpack was now bearing down on his shoulders. The last thing he wanted was more crap to deal with. Looking forward, their trail was a complete mess. Straight in front of them, covering the entire flat before they could push farther up the mountain, lay a massive pine tree that had taken down at least a dozen other trees with it when it had fallen. It completely blocked their trail

"Well, this wasn't here the last time we came through," Vin said.

"Yeah, there must have been one hell of a storm up here to do that. Though either way, we've gone too far now. We have to get past it," Ethan said.

"I sure am glad we weren't up here for that storm. I bet that was one crazy night," Vin said.

"Can you imagine the boom and crash that made when all of that came down?" Ethan said.

"Oh man, I bet you could have heard that clear down by the truck," Vin replied.

"Dude, that had to have sounded like you were right next to it down at the truck, anyone that was up here when that happened probably had the shit scared out of them," Ethan replied.

"I know it would have me," Vin said with a laugh. Vin began to walk forward, stepping onto the fallen trees. "I think if we are careful and take our time, we should be just fine getting over all of this stuff," Vin said.

Ethan looked down and checked the route on his GPS. He was just putting his GPS back in his pocket and getting ready to start crossing the trees when Vin called out, "Hey, you going to hurry the hell up?"

"Just hold your horses, I was just checking the route again. Last time we came through, this all wasn't down, I was just making sure we are on the right track," Ethan replied.

They made their way across the downed trees and worked around the still standing ones. It slowed them down a bit, but they were still able to stay close to pace. They reached the other side of the flat, then the mountain made a hairpin turn back to a very sharp incline. This would take them directly to the top of the mountain. The trees were starting to thin out, and Vin was starting to increase his pace.

As Vin sped up, he turned around, noticing that Ethan was not keeping up again. "Hey, you need me to slow down?" Vin asked.

"If you want to run up a mountain as fast as you can, that's all up to you," Ethan answered.

"It's not my fault that you're slow as hell," Vin said.

"Well, being as I am shorter than you, it takes me an extra minute to step over this shit. If you want to sprint your ass up this mountain, go right ahead. When I find you passed out on the side of the trail, I'll wait for you at the top," Ethan said.

The men finally reached the tree line. "This is the best part, remember?" Ethan said.

"Holy crap, this sucks. I'm damn glad we aren't going to leave this way; can you imagine having to pack an elk out on this trail?" Vin asked.

"Nope, and I sure don't want to," Ethan said.

This time, neither man took the lead. Both took a step at almost the exact same time. They wanted to stay close, this would be the most dangerous part of the hike. Any slips now could send them flying off the side of the mountain to their death. The trees were gone, and now it was just bare dirt and rocks. Their lungs began to burn. With every breath they tried to get as much air as they could, but they still hadn't gotten used to the elevation. Every step taken was harder than the one before. Looking up, they were headed for a low spot between the two peaks at the top. Their legs were on fire and sweat was pouring off their heads.

"Holy shit, dude, I have to take a breather," Ethan gasped, trying to catch his breath.

"I'm damn glad you caved because I was just about to myself. Good hell, this is a monster," Vin replied. Both men turned, putting their packs against the mountain, and collapsed to the ground, trying to catch their breath. "Just like the last time, this freaking sucks," Vin said.

"Yeah, but we have sure been through worse. At least it's not ninety-five degrees out here," Ethan replied.

"Hunting in the heat is an ass kicker for sure. That antelope hunt we did back when we were nineteen was unreal," Vin said.

"Okay, that one was a different story. We sure as hell didn't know what we were doing back then. It was the first week in September and taking off chasing them across the west desert wasn't our greatest idea. By the end of the second day, we ended up thirteen miles from the truck with no water in damn near ninety-degree heat," Ethan said.

"I'll have to say, that was the longest hike of my life. If we had been carrying that pint of whiskey with us back then, I sure as hell would have cracked the top," Vin said.

"Oh, for sure. I sure as hell thought we were both dead. If we hadn't had spare water in the truck, I still think we might not have made it back," Ethan said. Ethan pulled his legs back underneath him, placed a hand on the ground, and pushed himself back to his feet. "Come on, let's get this over with," he said as he pulled Vin up.

Gasping for air, Ethan was the first to break the crest of the summit. There was a wobble in both of his legs as he turned around. Vin was about ten steps behind him. Throwing out his hand, Ethan grabbed Vin and pulled him up to the flat. They stood there between the two shear peaks. In front of them was a strange, stepped plateau. They began to walk across, descending from the top step to the middle one where right smack dab between the peaks was a lake. Walking straight up to the edge, they both unbuckled their packs. Ethan sat down on a log while Vin found a nice rock with a flat top. They both sat in complete silence, trying to catch their breath. They stared across the lake, looking down over the range they were about to hike into.

"It has gotten us into trouble a few times, but taking off on foot like we do has sure let us see things no one else ever will," Vin said, breaking the silence.

Taking in Vin's comment, Ethan remained silent, staring into the lake. The water was crystal clear, not one impurity. "Well, I have to say, I know it is always amazing to fill our tags and get all of the meat, but this is what all the non-hunters will never understand. If we weren't hunting, there is no way we would have found this," Ethan said.

"Oh totally. If we weren't out here chasing elk, there would be no reason in the world to come up here," Vin said.

"Most people will never understand it is not just about killing an animal, it's about the adventure along the way," Ethan said. A silence filled the air again after Ethan's statement. Neither man said a word. Both sat there in complete silence, the only sound was a slight breeze winding between the peaks.

This was one of the moments that made all their insane trips worthwhile. They continued to sit there, taking in all they could see. Not only was it the beauty of the lake, the mountains, and the forest laid out in front of them, but the adventure they were about to have was right there. They were on a tight schedule, but for just a short while that didn't matter. They could see forever in every direction. Looking straight out at the mountain range in front of them, there it was. Cliff Lake. With a pair of binoculars, they could almost see the exact spot where they planned on setting up camp.

"If people would get off their four wheelers and hike more, they would get to see things like this," Vin said.

"True, but the best part of getting to see all this stuff is that eighty percent of people never will," Ethan replied. Ethan was the first to stand up, slowly putting his pack back on.

"Let's get going, we're only about halfway there now, and I really don't feel like setting up camp in the dark," Vin said as he stood up.

They began down the backside of the mountain. This side wasn't nearly as sharp of an angle as the side they had come up. Once they broke back into the trees, they tried to pick up the pace. They didn't travel as fast as they'd hoped they would, being that they were in completely untamed wilderness. They were the only men to have headed into this part of the forest for a long time. The trees were twice as thick as they had been on the other side of the mountain, and the entire floor of the forest was covered in dead fall. "Good hell, this stuff is a nightmare. I forgot about how terrible this side is," Ethan said.

"Get away from where all of the Fourth of July campers go and things get reclaimed by the forest," Vin replied.

There was a very slight marking of a trail from where the men had come through before. The day was fading fast, and when they could see that the sun was going down, they knew they were going to be arriving at camp in the dark. Checking their GPSs again, they made sure they were set on the tracking screen. After checking their trail, they took a quick stop to pull their head lamps out ahead of the sun fully setting. They didn't want to be caught in the dark unprepared. As they pushed through the forest, it didn't take much longer before they were covered in a blanket of darkness.

Their pace slowed to a crawl now that they were traveling by head lamp and GPS. "Maybe taking those couple of breaks wasn't the best idea we had, because hell, there went trying to get to camp before dark," Ethan said sarcastically.

"You say that like we have never hiked or arrived at camp so late before. There are countless times we have had to move in the dark," Vin replied.

"I don't care how many times we trek in the dark, it always sucks," Ethan said as he checked his GPS. "On that note, at least we are within a mile, so it shouldn't be long now."

It took them about another hour to reach Cliff Lake, breaking through the trees into a small clearing on the edge of the lake. Completely exhausted, both men dropped their gear; after the long day of hiking, it was the greatest feeling in the world. It felt as if thousands of pounds were taken off their shoulders. Scanning around with their lights, they found one of the small streams feeding into the lake. "That looks like as good of a spot as any," Vin said.

"I'm tired and hungry as hell. Let's get shit set up," Ethan said.

Vin and Ethan both pulled their own one-person tipi tent out of their packs and began to set them up. Each tent was set so they could use a small collapsible backpacking stove in it just in case the weather took a turn on them. After setting up his tent for the night, Ethan began to gather firewood as Vin pulled the food out. Once Ethan got the fire going, Vin began to cook dinner while Ethan went over to the small stream to refill their water.

A few minutes later, Vin and Ethan both sat down at the fire to eat dinner—freeze dried Mac and cheese. Ethan took the first bite. "Holy shit, after a day like this it wouldn't have mattered what in the hell this meal ended up being, this is the best meal I have ever had," Ethan said.

Vin smirked, "It always is. I'll never forget that batch of potatoes from a few years back. Holy shit, were they bad." Vin laughed

After they finished eating, Ethan began to relax and untied his boots, taking his socks off to let his feet breath. They sat across from each other, with a fire lighting up the night between them. There was a lot of cloud cover; the mountain range was as dark as the inside of a cave. The only spot breaking up the night was their fire. Surrounded by complete darkness, not knowing what could be wondering all around them, the warmth and light from the fire brought complete comfort.

Having his pants rolled up exposed the giant set of scars on Ethan's right calf. "So, you went with a dog bit you when you were a kid when you told Ashley the story, huh?" Vin said.

"Yup, that's the story," Ethan replied.

"I can't say that you weren't far off saying it was a dog. I mean you were kind of close," Vin said with a laugh.

"True, but still the wrong animal, and I wasn't exactly a kid when it happened," Ethan said.

"You ever tell anyone the true story?" Vin asked.

"Nope, and I don't plan on it," Ethan answered.

"I think with Kasey and Ashley, it's probably best that we take this one to the grave. They wouldn't be able to think straight anytime we take off to go hunt," Vin said.

"That's true, for sure."

Both paused for a second, just staring at the fire.

"You know, I still think about you not leaving me and hauling my ass out of those mountains," Ethan said.

"We have both been going on these crazy adventures since we could pee straight, you think for one minute that I would have left you up there?" Vin asked.

"No, but I do know that most people in this world would have," Ethan said.

"Yeah, and you would have been dead by the time I would have gotten back with anyone to help. In the end, hauling you out was the only real option that I had."

"We both could have died with you carrying me all the way back," Ethan replied. There was a long silence after Ethan said that.

Vin took a long breath, then he looked up at the coal black sky and over to the lake. "Well, I don't care what happens, it's our job to make sure we both get home safely. Come hell or high water," Vin said. "Now put that damn fire out and let's get to bed." Vin stood up, turning away from the fire and heading right for his tent.

Ethan wasn't in such a hurry though. He gazed the glow of the fire for a bit, then turned and stared at his right leg. The scars covered almost his entire calf. He couldn't believe he still had his leg let alone that he could walk normal. He didn't say anything as he sat there, reflecting in the glow of the fire. That had been their first real trip into the depths of the mountains. Vin had been twenty-one and Ethan just twenty. They never told anyone about the trip, the only evidence they even kept from that hunt was the one picture they each had hanging in their houses and the scars. Ethan just hoped that one day he would be able to repay the favor of Vin carrying him out of those mountains. *But how do you pay someone back for something like that?* The night was dead calm, not even a slight breeze rustled the air. Turning his head, Ethan saw that the lake was as still as a sheet of glass. There were only two sounds breaking the silence: the crackle of the fire and the close stream flowing into the lake. Ethan put his boots back on untied and walked over to the lake, filling up a water bottle. Standing on the edge of the lake, he took in a deep breath. The chilled air filled his lungs. He raised his right hand, running it under his hat, then down his face, and through his facial hair, exhaling slowly. He headed back, dumping the water on the fire, and then walked right to his tent preparing to go to sleep for the night.

Chapter 7

Early to Rise

A small beep from a wristwatch broke the silence of the morning. Ethan rolled over in his sleeping bag, turning off the alarm. Sitting up, he realized how sore his back was from the day before. He got dressed for the day quickly and began exiting his tent. It was still a few hours till daylight and still pitch black aside from a flame made from a small backpacking stove. Vin was already up and making himself a cup of coffee.

Vin turned his head to look at Ethan, "You want some?" He asked sarcastically.

"You know I can't stand that nasty shit," Ethan replied.

"Oh, I know, I just have to rub it in when I can," Vin laughed. Vin finished up his coffee and Ethan ate a quick protein bar and had some water. Once finished, they began to ready their gear for the day by stripping their daypacks off their big ones and packing up their essentials. They went over to the stream and filled their water containers with purified water. They then loaded the packs with gear to treat and process game if they were lucky enough to fill their tags this early. Each man also had a first aid kit, his own GPS, map and compass, spare jackets, a little extra ammo, all their optics, and emergency fire starters. They may have called these daypacks, but they readied the equipment so if they needed to stay away from camp for an extra two days, they would have the emergency equipment to do it.

They strapped on their daypacks, tightening them down. For optics, they each had one spotting scope, a pair of binoculars, a small monocular, and a range finder. Some of the equipment was old, but they had been starting to buy their gear when they were in their mid-teens. Their fathers taught them at a young age that quality gear would last them a long time. With their packs on and ready to go, both men bent down, picking up their rifles, and slinging them over their shoulders. "Just like always, things truly get started now," Vin said. Ethan took a drink out of his water bottle and turned back to Vin. "Well, let's see what we can find. We've got plenty of time, no reason to just jump on the first thing that we see. There's no one else up here," Ethan said.

"True. Let's get our asses on the move then," Vin replied. They set their head lamps back to the red light and began to hike for their first glassing spot. They had to make their way around the lake, then, according to their maps, a few miles from the lake was a meadow they were headed straight for. Making sure to move quickly but quietly, the men hurried through the forest. They needed to make it to the edge of the meadow well before sunrise to get set up.

They stayed in the trees trying to keep hidden. Vin was leading the way as they closed in on the last row of trees before the meadow. Turning his head back, he signaled to Ethan to come up the side next to him. "You see a nice place to set up?" Vin whispered.

Ethan didn't say a word, he just slowly turned his head, panning through the trees. On his second scan he stopped as he looked off to their left; he nudged Vin, pointing that way. There was a log lying in between two trees.

"Perfect," Vin whispered. Staying low, they quietly walked up to the log. They kneeled behind the cover, setting down their rifles and taking off their packs. It was still dark, but with this vantage point they would have full view of the whole meadow. Pulling out their binoculars, they wanted to have everything they would need ready before the sun rose.

Checking his watch, Ethan noticed that they still had a little over an hour before it would get light. "We've got plenty of time, so get comfortable," Ethan whispered, clicking off his headlamp. Now, with their red lights off, they were in the pitch black.

Turning to Ethan, Vin whispered, "I think we are going to have some luck here this morning. Being as last night was completely overcast, the animals should have stayed bedded down and didn't feed."

Ethan didn't say a word, he just nodded his head in agreement. As time passed, the sky began to light up, and the forest began to wake. Nothing knew they were there. A few birds began to move around as a tiny bit of light began breaking up the darkness. Hiding behind the log, Vin and Ethan pulled up their binoculars and began to scan the clearing.

These mornings were the best part of their hunting trips. It was the most amazing feeling in the world watching the forest wake. They could hear movement in the trees. It was just getting light enough for them to see. The sun was still behind the top of the mountain, but now the men were able to see that there was something walking in the gray haze that had formed over meadow. Both men lifted their rifles off the ground and positioned them leaning against the log. The sun rose higher, and they were able to make out what was in the meadow. Each man rested his gun while looking through his binoculars. Standing on the far side was a small herd of elk,.

"Looks like we have a little luck here," Ethan said.

"What do you think? I'm counting six," Vin said.

"That's what I have too, but I'm not seeing anything too big out there," Ethan replied. There were four cow elk and two small bulls, but the men weren't interested in going after either of the bulls.

"Let's just settle in for a while longer. See if anything else happens to wonder out," Vin said.

Time passed, and they never moved. The small herd finished feeding and moved out of the meadow.

"Well, what do you think?" Ethan asked.

"It's getting late enough in the morning that things are starting to bed down. I don't think anything else is going to be showing up until this evening unless something pushes them," Vin answered.

"Unless it's an animal, I don't think that there is something that's going to push them. Let's get the maps out and we can adjust our game plan for tonight and possibly tomorrow morning," Ethan said.

Vin pulled out his map and immediately marked the that they saw elk in the meadow there. At the same time, Ethan marked the spot on his GPS then proceeded to look at the map with Vin. They both looked over the map, setting up for where they would head next. "What about this right here?" Vin asked, pointing to a spot on the map.

"That's not exactly going to be a trip we can make and get back to camp for tonight," Ethan replied.

"According to the map there are a few good meadows up there and a really good water supply. I mean, we have the time to try it," Vin said.

"Once we get up there though, we will have to find a good spot to make a small camp site for the night. It's also probably going to be damn cold since we don't have the rest of our gear," Ethan replied.

"That's not a big deal, just keep a safe fire and we'll be just fine," Vin said.

"Hell, it wouldn't be the first time. Alright, let's get moving then."

They put their gear away, leaving out one map and their compasses. Setting a heading, they now had their plan.

Loading up their packs and grabbed their rifles for the next leg of their journey. They'd have to cover a lot of ground quickly, but it was doable. They pushed through the dense woods, moving farther into the mountain range. Vin and Ethan examined the map and their surroundings very closely to make sure that they were in the right spot—they were. They would have to ascend higher up the mountain, hiking through a steep meadow. To their left, the clearing ran right into a rock wall, a good-sized stream flowing down from the top of the mountain between them. To the right, a wall of trees started again, running straight up to the treeline at a sheer angle. There was a small portion of the trees that flattened off with the meadow.

"That sure as hell looks like it's our way up there," Ethan said.

"Look at it this way, it's not near as bad as our hike over that first mountain," Vin replied, stepping forward, the first to begin the climb up the mountain.

Ethan stood there, looking up at what lie before them. He let out a small laugh, "The shit we end up getting into," he muttered to himself.

"Hey, you coming?" Vin yelled back at Ethan.

Not saying a word, Ethan adjusted his pack and began following Vin. The small clearing of trees on the steep side of the mountain would take them up to a giant, flat valley surrounded by mountains. Unless they wanted to scale more mountains or battle through an extremely dense wall of trees, this would be the only way up and down.

Sweat raced down the sides of their heads, their lungs burning. "Holy shit, my shins are all but numb," Ethan said as he broke the crest of the incline, dropping to a knee and taking a second to catch his breath.

"Oh hell, it wasn't that bad," Vin said, trying to catch his breath as well.

"That's why you're not huffing and puffing either?" Ethan shot back.

Standing back up, they both saw the clearing run out in front of them before once again smacking into a wall of trees. Checking the time, Ethan could see it was now middle of the afternoon.

"We need to get a move on to scout out that meadow," Vin said as he started walking again with Ethan right behind him. It took another two hours for them to reach the far edge of the meadow. They picked up on a game trail right away.

"You see anything?" Ethan asked.

"There are a lot of tracks, and they all look like they are from this morning," Vin replied.

"Yeah, but I don't see any elk around," Ethan said.

"Let's move over there and set up again," Vin said pointing off to their right.

It didn't take long for a creature to wander past them. Ethan nudged Vin, "Look," he whispered.

Lowering his binoculars, Vin turned to Ethan, "Holy shit, dude! They're coming out of the trees like ants!" A massive heard of elk emerged from the treeline.

"There are at least three massive six points in there," Ethan said.

"What time you got?" Vin asked.

"We have about an hour and a half till it gets dark, and night's going to come fast."

"Shit, we don't know where we're going to camp for the night. There's no way we will get a stock on in that time. You got this marked on your GPS?" Vin said.

"You know it," Ethan replied.

"Are you thinking what I'm thinking?"

"Yup, let's get camped for the night and get a few different plans in the work," Ethan said.

Vin nodded his head as they quietly snuck away from the meadow.

They left the meadow and headed toward the base of one of the peaks, not wanting to camp in the area they would be hunting in. Once they got to the base of the peak, they found a rocky overhang that looked like a great place to camp. "What do you think of that?" Ethan asked.

"For tonight, it might as well be Caesar's palace. Just please try to refrain from spooning with me," Vin replied.

Ethan went to grab firewood as Vin started to break camp. The outcrop went back into the base of the mountain, providing almost perfect shelter. It had an overhang and, with it being back into the mountain, two rock sides. The front even had a few fallen boulders blocking the entrance as well. Once Ethan returned, Vin had everything set and ready for a fire and was beginning to prepare a small meal from their extra food.

It was a dark, overcast night. Without any light, Ethan couldn't see his hand in front of his face. "With how overcast tonight and last night have been, we have to be due for a storm here soon," Ethan said.

"Don't jinx us. If we get a storm, it's going to screw us over for tomorrow," Vin replied. Their small fire gave off a glow throughout the forest, radiating heat in their outcrop of rocks. After the long day the men had, the heat of the fire on their hands and faces was the best feeling they'd had since leaving for the mountains. They each prepped a freeze-dried meal for dinner.

"As long as it just stays overcast and we don't get a storm, we could get really lucky with those elk heading back to the meadow in the morning," Ethan said.

"Oh, trust me, I have my fingers crossed. While you were collecting firewood, I did a little mapping. I have a few different routes planned, pending on weather and the wind," Vin said

"Sounds like a plan." Ethan threw another long on the fire. "Well, I'm going to get some rest," he said. Vin laid down across the fire from Ethan and fell asleep as well. The fire had burned down to coals, the glow all but gone now, and the darkness had begun to consume the forest all around them.

As the men slept, a chill came in the air, and the forest had become completely still. It had become one of the nights on the mountain where anything moving could be heard. It was dead calm. However, there was one creature on the move that night. Back down the mountain by Cliff Lake, one very dim light moved on the forest floor. It moved so slowly and quietly through the forest that not even the crunch of a leaf or a twig breaking was heard. The light moved closer to the lake so smoothly that not one bird or animal stirred at its approach. The light reflected off the water as a middle-aged man wearing a small dim headlamp knelt beside it. The man had long, greasy hair past his shoulders and a long beard down to the middle of his chest. For a man his age, he was in top physical condition. His camouflage was old and faded, and he carried an old, torn backpack and an extremely worn rifle with marks of rust down the barrel and scratches and dents covering an almost completely unfinished wooden stock.

The man filled his canteen in the lake. As he stood, he caught the smell of ashes from the previous night's fire. Turning away from the lake, he walked right to the camp. Shinning his light around the campsite, he headed for the tents first, taking stalk of the gear the men had left until their return. Standing there, the man let out a relaxing breath and smiled. *I didn't think they would come this far into my mountains*, he thought. *I'm going to have to make sure they don't find anything.*

Chapter 8

The Hunt Begins

The man searched through everything that the two hunters had stored at the main camp, finding their bigger backpacks. He stole anything that could be made useful to him—the extra food, batteries, and extra survival supplies. He repacked the gear he didn't want and added weight by placing rocks in the bags. Picking up each pack, he walked over to the edge of the lake and with one swift throw, the fancier of the packs flew from his hands and smashed into the surface of the water. He grabbed the second pack and quickly tossed it through the air and into the lake as well. Both packs sank to the bottom, taking all the hunter's spare gear with them.

The man decided to leave the shelters up considering that there was no point in destroying them now that they were completely empty. Searching around the edge of the camp, even in the complete dark, he was able to find the hunter's footprints. The prints showed where the men left the camp and circled around the other side of the lake. Once he noticed the direction they were traveling, a smile grew across his face. *This is quite convenient, this is the way I was going anyway,* he thought to himself. He stood and began to track the two men. Even though the night was pitch black and he only had his small headlamp, the man still had an easy time following the trail the men had left. Spending the rest of the night following their path through the forest, it was just a few hours before daylight when he found himself sitting in the exact spot on the edge of the meadow where the men had waited, watching the small herd of elk.

Vin and Ethan had been awake for a while. They had eaten a small breakfast and were getting their gear on. As Ethan finished lacing up his boots, Vin pulled out his map. "Alright, what's the plan for today?" Ethan asked.

"We have a few options. Obviously, the simplest plan would be to go right back to where we were last night," Vin said.

"Simplest, yes, but we would end up being up wind from them," Ethan said.

"For sure, they'll wind us right away, and we won't even have a chance. But I think I found us a different path that we can use to get on the other side. Then we'll be down wind," Vin replied.

"That would, of course, be the best option. Show me what you're thinking," Ethan said, moving closer to look over the map.

Vin moved his hand across the map, showing Ethan what looked like a narrow pathway to skirt the mountain and get on the backside of the meadow. Folding up the map Vin turned to Ethan, "So what do you think?"

"It's the best move that we are going to have," Ethan said, pulling on his pack. Having all their gear on, they both stepped from the outcrop and looked up. "Can't see a star in the sky. I hope this doesn't mean what I think it means," Ethan said.

"Don't say it, whatever you do, don't say it," Vin replied.

"I'm just saying there is a chance for rain today," Ethan replied with a smirk.

"Damn it, damn it, damn it. You just had to say it and jinx us, didn't you? We didn't hike our happy asses all the way up this damn mountain so that we could have some stupid bad luck hit us," Vin shot back, picking up his rifle and holding it in the ready position.

Ethan chuckled. "To hell with a stupid jinx. Shit happens. If a little rain is the worst thing that happens up here, we'll be doing pretty good," Ethan said.

"Really? You have to double down on it now?" Vin asked.

Ethan let out another laugh, "You going to lead the way, or am I? We have ground to cover."

Vin slowly shook his head as he slung his rifle over his shoulder, "Come on, let's get going and hope the weather holds out," As Vin turned to walk away, he stopped at the first tree he came to and raised his left hand balled up in a fist. He then proceeded to knock on the trunk of the tree.

Not far behind him, Ethan watched. "Better safe the sorry, right?" Ethan asked.

"You bet your ass it is," Vin answered.

When they were about halfway to the meadow, a slight breeze picked up, and Ethan could smell a change in the air. "You smell that?" Ethan asked.

"It sure smells like rain, doesn't it?" Vin replied.

"We'll just have to keep trucking and see what happens. There is no point in turning back now," Ethan said.

Continuing to push on, it wasn't long before a light rain began to fall. But the rain wasn't the problem. The direction of the wind had changed with the start of the storm coming in.

"Get under some cover and let's get the map out," Vin said. They quickly found a tree and pulled out the map, looking over their options. With the wind changing, I don't think it will be a bad idea to head back and go the direction that we took yesterday," Vin said.

"I think you're getting ahead of yourself. You're forgetting something," Ethan said.

"What's that?" Vin asked.

"Once this storm settles in, the wind will stop. I think we should modify our trail right here," Ethan said, pointing to a section on the map. "See the stream here? We can see about finding a good point to cross, and maybe buy us a little bit of time with the wind. It will also set us up right behind the meadow,"

Vin pulled out his GPS and compass, then began to set a heading on both, "I think we should be able to make that work. Though if we can't cross that stream, it'll be what could wreck this plan," Vin said.

"Weren't you just telling me to stay positive a little while back? Now you're the one saying things like that? Why can't you just stay positive?" Ethan said sarcastically.

Shaking his head, Vin just folded up the map and looked back at Ethan, "Come on, let's go."

Vin led the way as Ethan brought up the rear, tracking their progress on his map, making sure to navigate so they would stay on course. They swung a wide path through the thick forest, trying to hang far away from the meadow, not wanting to scare anything away that might be feeding there or let anything have the chance of smelling them. Eventually, they came across the stream that flowed through the high valley. "Okay, this isn't quite the little stream we thought it was on the map," Vin said.

"Yeah, I was hoping that it was going to be something we could easily walk through," Ethan replied.

"Oh, we could walk through it. It would just be at least waist high, and that water is going to be damn cold," Vin said.

"Better pick a good spot to cross, or we are going to be changing our plans and priorities very quickly," Ethan said.

Taking their time here, they made sure to pick a good safe place to cross. They found a spot with a few big rocks and a downed tree trunk. Ethan was to cross first, being extra careful to make sure to step up onto the rocks. The stream flowed slow enough that he may have been able to wade to the other side, but it flowed fast enough that one missed step and he could easily be swept away. As Ethan was just starting to step off the first rock, he heard Vin comment, "You slip and fall in here, and I will have a hell of a time trying to come find you this time." Ethan looked back, giving him a sarcastic "shut up" look and headed across the stream.

Ethan was just about safely to the other side when Vin began to relax and look around. That's when he saw something. Something that was very out of place at the base of a tree a little bit away from the stream. Since leaving the main trail they hadn't seen any sign of another person having been back into this area of the mountain range. Vin walked over to the tree, bending to one knee, and reached down to pick up a broken old cell phone. "How did you get all the way out here?" Vin muttered to himself.

Standing up and looking ahead, Vin could see Ethan waiting for him on the other side. Not wanting to be loud, Ethan he was using his arms to signal for Vin to hurry up and get across so they could get moving. Standing back from the stream, Vin could see that something wasn't right about it. Now, looking at it this way, the crossing looked very out of place. Staring at the big rocks, he could tell they had always been there, but it was the tree trunk that was out of place. There wasn't a tree stump anywhere nearby. As a matter of fact, there weren't any points on the trunk that showed it had broken off and fallen over. Vin's mind began to wonder how it came to be placed right there.

Vin slid the broken phone into his pocket and crossed the stream as fast as he could.

Stepping off the tree trunk, Ethan immediately grabbed him to see what had taken him so long, "Hey, what did you find over there?".

Vin reached into his pocket and pulled out the broken phone.

"How in the hell do you figure that made its way clear up hear?" Ethan asked.

"I have no idea, but it sure has been up here and while," Vin replied.

"Well, if I were a betting man, which I totally am, I'd say it's been here at least eight years. I mean, when was the last time someone packed around a flip phone?" Ethan said.

"I would say we got rid of ours back when we were in college at the latest. Not only that, but did you notice,"

"Um, have you noticed the bottom of that log place there?" Ethan asked, cutting Vin off.

Vin turned around and look at the base to see what Ethan was talking about. The base of the trunk had crossed saw marks on it. "I noticed from the other side that the log almost looked like it was placed there to be a bridge," Vin said.

A silence fell over both men, but they could tell what the other was thinking and the words not said aloud. What or who had put that log in its place? "Well, we don't have time to worry about that. We have to get back to the meadow. The smell of rain is getting strong, and I have a feeling it's going to be quite the storm," Vin said.

Turning around and beginning to head back on course towards the meadow, Vin was back in front, leading the way with Ethan just a few steps behind him. As Vin walked away from the crossing, his uneasy feeling didn't seem to leave, but in fact got worse. He peered over his shoulder looking back. It almost felt as if a black cloud had settled in on top of him, and the feeling that he was being watched was back. *Someone had to have built that crossing. The phone might be old, but that tree had been put there within the last few months.* Vin's mind was racing in all different direction with these thoughts. They pushed closer and closer to the point where they were going to set up on the edge of the meadow, but Vin's mind kept circling back to everything that they had come across. He kept his head on a swivel. They had been the only sign of humans on this entire side of the mountain, but then they came across what he considered to be a maintained river crossing. Something wasn't adding up.

The older man was just reaching the top of at the top of the hill where the valley started. He was following the hunter's trail almost step for step. With every few steps he would bend down, checking the trail, and his long, greasy hair would swing forward, covering half of his face. He would tilt his head up after checking the ground, looking out of the top of his eyes. He slowly cranked his head around, checking his surroundings before standing back up. He didn't make a sound. Moving along the trail, he never missed one single movement that the hunters took, all the while knowing everything that was going on around him.

The night before, he had tracked the hunters right to the point where they had peered through the trees to spot for elk. Looking the area over, he could even tell where the men had sat, recognizing the location as a glassing point. It hadn't taken him long that morning to find the trail that took him right to the spot where the men set up their camp. Just as he was about to reach the rock outcrop it began to rain. It was a steady rain, and it didn't take long for the top of the ground to form a layer of mud.

Walking up on the shelter, he could see one trail going into cover and one leaving. The one leaving lead deeper into the mountain range. The water from the rain dripped off the man as he examined the camp site. He could smell their fire from the night before and could make out exactly where they had laid out the sleeping bags and slept. He could even tell right where they had eaten, too.

The man was very methodical in how he studied the camp. He stayed in the cover of the rocks while the rain moved from light and steady to a heavy downpour, using the time to study every detail the camp site could give him. He smiled once more, looking straight out from underneath the outcrop, taking in the surrounding woods. Looking just off to his left, the man saw a spot about two hundred and fifty yards from where he was standing. It was slightly elevated from where he was now. There were two trees with a slight gap between them and just a little bit of cover around the bottom. His smile grew bigger as he thought to himself, *If I have to return here later, that will be the perfect spot.* He turned his gaze forward again, stepping out into the rain, and following the trail that these two men had given him. He knew he was getting closer; it was time to figure out why these two men were on his mountain.

Vin and Ethan were sitting on the edge of the meadow, both tucked tight in the tree line. They had put a little distance between them this time to ensure that they had a full view of the meadow. Ethan was seated at the base of a tree with his rifle resting across his lap and his binoculars in one hand, and Vin was off to the left, kneeling behind a downed tree, his rifle resting against the log. Vin leaned his elbows on the log as he surveyed the meadow through his binoculars. It hadn't started to rain yet when they had reached the meadow, but now they found themselves sitting in a complete downpour.

Ethan got up on his feet and snuck over to where Vin was set up. "Hey, you know we saw that big bull for just a few moments after we got set up," Ethan said.

"Yeah, but he didn't give us a shot," Vin replied.

"Well, now that we are caught in this storm, let's get back to our spot to camp and try to get dry. The elk aren't going to be moving about in this mess," Ethan said.

"Agreed. But once we get dried off, let's head back down to our main camp. We now know where the bulls we're looking for are. We can go get re-geared up before we come back after them," Vin said.

"Good call. We have the time, and as long as we don't pressure them, they should stay around here," Ethan replied.

Vin and Ethan made sure to get moving quickly, but the rain was beating down now, and the ground had become a slick and sticky mud. With each step, their feet would sink, the mud wrapping around the top of their boots. They quickly made their way to the point of the stream where they had crossed before. "Hey, Vin, this water has risen like crazy. What do you think?" Ethan asked.

Vin scanned around, looking the crossing up and down. "I'm not sure. That water is right at the top of the rocks we crossed on," Vin said.

"One slip and we are headed down stream in a bad way," Ethan replied.

"Shit. Let's head up stream and see if we can find a better point," Vin answered, turning and making his journey the other way.

Ethan adjusted his pack, fixed his rifle over his shoulder, and was right on Vin's heels as they headed up stream.

At first, they hiked on the edge of the now violently flowing stream. Vin was trying to find a place to cross, leading the way and making sure to stay close to the edge. They both trudged through the slick mud that only got worse the longer it stormed. Vin's foot caught a slight angle, and he slipped down on his shoulder. Splashing mud and water all around himself, he began to slide toward the stream. Ethan was right behind Vin when he slipped, and he quickly dropped down to a knee and swung his hand out, hooking the top strap on Vin's pack, stopping his fall right as his feet began to touch the water. Ethan did manage to stop Vin's descent, though with Vin's weight pulling him down, Ethan began to slide as well. Ethan flung his other hand out, grabbing a tree branch. Ethan had one hand wrapped around Vin's pack and the other grasping a tree for dear life. Ethan curled his wrist in, using every muscle in his upper body to pull them both away from the water. If not for the branch, they both would have slid right into the stream.

"Well, that was close enough to make your butt pucker," Vin said in a low voice as his body shook.

"Let's put a little more room between us and the stream now," Ethan replied.

"Good call. I got a little lax on that one. We will make sure to leave that part out when we get back home," Vin said.

"Yeah, I think that's a good idea," Ethan answered.

They made sure to put some distance between them and the stream, staying away from the bank and higher up on the flat. Now, they weren't in any close danger of sliding back down.

"Chalk one up for you, buddy. Now you had to pull my ass out of the fire," Vin said as he continued to make their way through the woods.

Ethan gave a half-hearted laugh at the comment, "I don't think that was quite up to the level of my incident," Ethan said.

"Oh hell, it wasn't that big of a deal, dude. It would have turned out the exact same if it had been me rather than you," Vin said.

Ethan didn't reply to that comment, he just followed close behind Vin, but as they continued to hike, the comment sunk in more and more. As he walked, he glanced down at his leg. The accident started to flash through his head again. Yes, he may have just kept Vin from sliding into the stream, but it wasn't even close to what Vin had done for him.

At this point, the rain had become brutal, and neither Vin nor Ethan had one thing on them that was dry at all. "Ethan, keep your eyes open for a good spot to stop, we need to just find some cover and get out of this rain. If it turns cold on us with everything being this wet, we'll be screwed and could easily become hypothermic," Vin said.

"I was already trying to find a spot. Let's turn a little farther into the forest, we might have some better luck there. I think we will just end up seeing more of the same if we stay this close to the water," Ethan replied. Pushing farther into the trees, they turned their attention away from looking for a place to cross, to trying to find some shelter to get dry. Now that they were just pushing blindly into the forest, Ethan pulled his GPS out of his pocked making sure that it was still tracking their position; the last thing they needed to do now was get lost.

As the time passed, they slowly began to realize that they were now in the middle of the valley, probably up on the flat. "Hey, I don't think we're going to find another outcrop like we did last night," Ethan shouted.

Stopping, Vin turned around, "I hate to say it, but I think your right. Let's change our thought process here. Keep an eye out for anything that could provide cover," Vin said.

"Can do. Though it will probably just be a tree," Ethan said.

They kept an eye out for anything as they continued through the forest, but with how hard it was raining, even the trees were not going to provide any cover at all. It was beginning to occur to them both that they were going to have to start building a shelter soon. Just as they were about ready to break down and start building, they came across something they never would have expected.

Chapter 9

The Cabin

"Hold up one second," Vin said. He peered into the trees in front of them, trying to figure out what he thought they had found.

Ethan walked up to his side, completely baffled. He pulled out his binoculars to try and get a better look. "Holy shit, you're not going to believe this," Ethan said.

"Is it what I think it is?" Vin asked.

"You just have to look. You won't believe it unless you see it for yourself," Ethan answered.

Vin pulled out his binoculars to look for himself. "That almost looks like a trapper camp from the 1800s," Vin said.

"Should we go check it out?"

"Dude, we're alone in the mountains with no way to get in contact with anyone for help. Wouldn't you say that is the plot of every horror movie that you have ever seen?" Vin said.

"You have a point, but good hell, what else are we supposed to do? I mean, we both have guns and know how to handle our shit. And it will get us out of the rain; I am pretty damn sick of being sopping wet," Ethan said.

"Well, why the hell not? Let's go for it."

The camp was a hundred and fifty yards away. Over all the years that they had been hunting they had come across a lot of crazy things in the woods, but this was unlike anything they had ever seen before. As curious as they both were, the closer they got, the faster their hearts raced. It looked as if it shouldn't have been there, and as they began to close the gap, it became obvious that it wasn't just a normal makeshift shelter that some other hunter had quickly thrown up. Whoever had built this had really settled in.

It was a sealed cabin, and the owner had even made a stone chimney coming off the back. They approached the front of the cabin. Picking up his hand, Ethan touched the front wall. "I can't believe it. This can't be real," he said removing his hand and walking to the corner of the cabin. Slowly, he turned the corner, exposing the rest of the camp. Vin was on his heals. Their eyes widened and mouths dropped open. Neither man could catch his breath as they saw what was laid out before them. Behind the main cabin was a lean-to shed. Running along the top of the shed were struts with ropes wrapped around them. Meat hooks hung on the end of the ropes. Walking past the lean-to they saw an enclosed smaller shed. Ethan walked up to the door, grabbing the handle. Ethan's eyes widened and his jaw fell open once more as he got a look inside. Reaching back, he snapped his fingers. "Um, Vin get over here," Ethan said.

Walking up, Vin looked around the shed. "Hell no!" he said shocked.

They both were staring into a fully stocked food storage. There was everything from dried meat to canned food. Ethan closed the door and they slowly and silently backed away. No wind blew through the forest, all they could hear was the sound of the rain beating against the ground.

They split up to check out the rest of the camp and met back up in the middle. "I can't believe this place. You don't just find things like this," Vin said.

"I honestly don't know what to say. I mean, my grandfather told me about seeing places like this when he was a kid," Ethan said.

"So did mine, but that would have been in the early 1900s. Back then, there were people that still lived like this," Vin said.

"What in the hell is this place?" Ethan asked.

"I couldn't have imagined it. I would say we have stumbled across an old cabin, but look at this," Vin said as he walked back to the cabin.

Ethan looked up and scanned his eyes around the roof before walking around the back and examining the chimney. Vin circled the cabin one more time before joining Ethan back by the chimney. "This whole camp is being maintained. Look at this, the cabin is completely sealed; the roof doesn't have one leak in it," Ethan said. Both men paused, staring out at the camp, trying to take it all in.

"Someone is living here." As Vin spoke his voice began to crack in fear. Slowly, he turned his head and scanned the tree line around them.

"I hate to say this, but I'm not seeing any other option for us to try and get out of the rain. So, I have to ask, do we dare duck in for a few minutes to get out of this storm?" Ethan asked.

They stood in place, neither man wanting to make the final call. Then Vin turned, taking the first step toward the front of the cabin. Ethan followed just behind him.

Vin reached forward and grabbed a stick that was fastened from the door to the wall of the cabin, locking the door in place. Not having any hinges, the door rested on the ground. The top and the bottom corners of the door were loosely tied to the wall of the cabin with a strap of leather which gave it enough clearance to move. A hole had been knocked through the door for a handle and a few sticks had been joined in a U shape to lock the door to the wall. A stop had been built underneath the door to keep it from falling. Holding the door up once he lifted the handle, Vin pushed on it, sliding the door across the ground before it got wedged stuck. Reaching around, Vin grabbed the door, picking it up from the ground, unwedging it and throwing it open. An ice-cold chill shot through both of their bodies paralyzing them in fear as they took their first glimpse inside the cabin.

The inside was dark because there were no windows to let any light in. There was just one small dim beam of light at the back of the cabin coming in through the fireplace. Vin and Ethan both pulled a flashlight out of their pockets as they walked inside. They closed the door behind them, trying to do everything they could to keep the weather out. Using the flashlights, they began scanning the space. "What in the actual hell is this?" Ethan asked.

"This wasn't built this year or even last year, this place has been perfected over a long period of time," Vin said.

There was a makeshift bed not too far from the fireplace. Ethan walked over and sat down on it to see how it felt. "I have to say, for living out here, this is a damn comfy bed," he said.

In the middle of the cabin was a crudely made table with a seat for one person. Vin made his way to look it over, "Whoever this was, the guy was a hell of a craftsman." The chair was carved out of a stump and even had a back rest on it, and the table was the size of an average coffee table and didn't have one give of wiggle.

Standing up, Ethan walked over to the fireplace where a big carved chair rested right in front. "Does this guy really have a custom-made man chair for himself?" Ethan asked, shocked.

Continuing to look over the inside, there were forms of built-in storage and a place to prep food on a wooden countertop. "Can you even believe this?" Vin asked. They were continuing their study of the cabin when Ethan caught a quick glimpse of something catching the beam of his flashlight from under the bed

"Hold the phone, do you see that?" Ethan pointed in the item's direction. Dropping down to the side of the bed, he blindly reached underneath it. His fingers caught on a handle and he began to pull what ended up being a footlocker from under the bed, "This could explain a lot about this place to us."

"Correction, that could explain everything about this place," Vin said, stepping forward. He knelt and lifted the footlocker, setting it on the table. "Hmm, no lock."

"Wouldn't have a need for one out here. What does it matter?" Ethan said.

Vin gave a shrug, acknowledging what Ethan had said before sliding the closing latch to the side and pulling the top back. The locker let out a rusty creek and as Vin lifted the top, resting it all the way open. The locker contained two sliding drawers, one off to the left and one to the right. In the drawer to the right were maps—maps of every mountain range that was even close to the area. Looking through the maps, there were notes written down the sides and tops. All the notes corresponded with drawings he had made on them. Each map had spots that were circled. In fact, not only were there circles, but there were arrows and X's drawn on other areas on the maps as well. Every marking on them was pointing to something, but what that was or why they didn't know yet.

"Holy shit. Look at this. Each map has one spot marked on it in the same way," Vin said as he flipped through the multiple maps.

"What do you think that means?" Ethan asked.

"Honestly, it looks like whoever owns this cabin has at least four or five other camps throughout all these mountain ranges. Whoever this is, he is living in the mountains year-round, moving from place to place. It looks like he's been here for quite some time, I mean look, this map is dated from almost twenty years ago. Do you think this is just some crazy mountain man that wanted to live off the grid?" Vin said.

"Well, um, I think this just might have gone from bad to worse," Ethan said. Ethan had moved from poking through the right drawer over to the left. There was a paper on the front that blocked the contents of what was in it. Lying underneath the paper was a pile of ID's, from driver's licenses to student ID's.

"What the hell?" Vin looked over, his eyes wide. The paralyzing fear had returned now, and their bodies had become completely numb. Neither one of them wanted to move a muscle.

Please, God, please tell me this isn't real, Ethan thought to himself. He forced his hands to reach
for the ID's, feeling like his heart was about to explode. His hands were shaking so badly that he didn't have any idea if he could even hold onto anything. He reached into the pile, picking up a hand full.

    Vin peered over from looking at the maps as Ethan began to look through the ID's. "Wait, I recognize that one," Vin said.

    Ethan turned his head slowly. His eyes were so wide now that they looked like they were going to burst from his head. "What in the hell did you just say?" Ethan asked.

    "Yeah, I remember seeing that guy on the news about five years ago." As Vin spoke, fear had crept into his voice. "He went missing for a few months. They eventually found his body twenty-five miles from where he disappeared. The news said that it looked like he was mauled by a bear."

    Ethan continued through the pile, but it didn't take long before he stopped again. This time, the fear filled Ethan's voice, "Do you recognize these two?"

    Vin closed his eyes, dropping his head to his chest as he took a step back. "Damn it. Yes, I do," he answered.

    "This couple went missing two years ago about a hundred miles from here in one of the ranges on those maps," Ethan said.

"Yeah, they were found at the bottom of a cliff. The news said that search and rescue had figured they had gotten lost and fell off the side of the mountain," Vin said.

"I don't know about you, but I think we found something really—and I mean really—bad here," Ethan said.

"It's getting closer to looking that way," Vin replied.

Ethan moved those two ID's to the side. He continued shuffling through the stack, some of the cards were a lot older, a few even went back fifteen or even eighteen years. Each time he found an ID of someone they had seen on the news for having gone missing in the woods, a lump in his throat got bigger. Then Ethan came to the last one and his mouth fell open and his eyes about jumped out of his head.

Vin looked over and dropped everything that he was holding as his hands started to shake.

"Holy shit, that's the guy from the missing poster in the store," Ethan said as he battled to deal with the shaking in his voice. Both men were in complete shock. Ethan turned to Vin, but Vin couldn't muster any words for a few moments. "This guy is a serial killer and he's been making it look like people have just been going missing in the woods for like fifteen or twenty years," Ethan said.

Vin carefully pulled the top drawers out of the locker, exposing the bottom. There was a wallet inside, and Ethan reached down to grab it. Opening the wallet, Ethan saw that the driver's license was still inside. He pulled the ID out, "Flint Jones. Do you think he was another one of his victims?" Ethan asked.

Vin didn't answer as he reached into the bottom as well. There was a small leather-bound book at the bottom. Picking it up, Vin untied the binding, opened to the first page, and began to read it out loud. "October 18th, 1997, I abandoned my truck at the road. I have no plans on ever returning to it. This world has beat me, robbed me, and hated me from the time I was born. Everyone was frightened of me. Why? Because they said I was weird. That's what they said at first, then it turned to them saying I was violent and crazy. Once Ryan became scared of me and abandoned me, his family had gone around telling everyone I was insane. They just didn't understand. Then Mom started believing it too. I was only seventeen when she threw me out, claiming that I was scaring her and that I was just like my dad. Well, her mistake was comparing me to him. Every one of them can go to hell. I'm done with people, and I'm not coming back this time. These mountains are about to become mine." Vin stopped reading and turned to Ethan, "I think that's him." Vin said, his voice cracking.

"Flip through and read some more," Ethan said.

Skipping about a third of the way forward through the journal, Vin began to read again. "April 9th, 2005, I came here to escape from people, but they keep finding me. They should know this is my home and to stay the hell out of here. Two college kids were at my lake fishing. That's my damn lake, they have no right to come to my home and steal from me! Once I found them and their camp, they didn't stand a chance . . . they never do." Vin paused.

Ethan reached over, closing the journal. He felt as if he was going to throw up. "Don't read anymore, we got our answer," he said.

Standing there in complete silence, time seemed to have stopped. Neither man knew what to do or say.

Vin was finally able to shake things off. "How long have we been here?" he asked.

There was a pause.

"I think we've been here longer than we should have been," Ethan whispered.

"We need to get out of these mountains and report this. You remembered your camera, right?" Vin asked.

"It's in my pack," Ethan answered as he swung off the pack and began digging through it.

"Alright, we need to take pictures of all of this. If we don't have evidence, there is no way in hell anyone will believe us," Vin said

Pulling out the camera, Ethan started to take pictures of everything he could—how the inside of the cabin was laid out, the stack of ID cards. They unfolded the maps and took detailed photos of everything Flint had drawn and written on them. "Let's get outside, take a few of the camp, and get this wrapped up," Ethan said. The storm hadn't let up at all, it was still a down pour, and there was standing water all around the camp. Their feet splashed in the mud and water as Ethan began to walk around, taking photos of the camp. He quickly snapped a few photos of the front and around the sides, making sure to show the whole thing in detail.

"Okay, I think I've gotten all that I can get," Ethan said.

Vin grabbed the camera from Ethan and placed it back in his pack for him. "While you were taking photos, I marked where we are on the map as well as the GPS. With the location and the photos of the camp we should have plenty of proof. Let's get the hell out of here before whoever lives here shows up and we have to deal with him," Vin said.

"Agreed. But we didn't find anywhere else to cross the stream. Are we just going to try it at the log then?" Ethan asked.

"I hate to say it, but I think that's our only option," Vin answered.

"Well, then let's just get this over with and get going," Ethan said.

They both readjusted their packs and swung their rifles off their shoulders, checking to make sure they had a live round in the chamber, and keeping the guns in the ready position. Vin started to walk ahead, his head on a swivel, scanning the forest for anything that looked out of place. Ethan turned around as Vin walked forward, slowly backing out of the camp, making sure to check everything that was behind them. He had goose bumps running down both his arms and across his neck. He and Vin both knew what it felt like to be followed or even hunted before, but nothing like this. Nothing that could hunt them and think like they could. Ethan took about ten steps backward, turned without stopping, and continued behind Vin. With one more look over his shoulder, he headed off into the woods, making sure to keep his head on a swivel.

With all the photos that they took and searching they had done, there was one thing that the men had missed. In the woods to the side of the cabin, Flint knelt to the side of a tree. His military boonie hat was soaked with water, and he wore an old camouflage poncho. Peering through a new pair of binoculars, he watched as the men finished documenting his cabin and back into the woods. He had gotten to the area as they had finished taking the pictures. They didn't know it, but there was another way to cross the stream about another mile up from where they were. Flint had come home by one of his other routes. He had seen the direction that they had gone and known that it would put them in the vicinity of his cabin. His way was shorter and got him to the cabin quicker. Now, as Flint was watching them in the trees, he could see he had made the right decision.

Looking through the binoculars he was able to watch as the shorter man backed away. The man was almost staring right at the spot Flint was watching them from. He slowly lowered the binoculars as the men walked off into the forest. A smile grew across his face.

Despite his smile, Flint had grown quite infuriated. Not only did he now know who he had been following, but they had found his home. *Now they know where I live. They probably found the evidence of everyone that I have killed in the last twenty years and saw the maps of my camps and everywhere I go. They made their way far enough into the backcountry that they can survive on their own out here.* His hands began to tighten into fists as his entire body tensed up. Flint began to take deep breaths.

They came onto my mountain. They trespassed on my property. Now I find them in my home taking photos of my stuff. I can't — no I won't — let this happen. They have to pay. There is no way in hell I am going to let them out of my mountains. I'm going to kill them both, but this time they are just going to disappear. I will never let anyone know what happened to them. These men will never know what hit them, Flint thought to himself. His smile grew bigger. Flint threw his backpack back on, then proceeded to put his rifle at the ready. Hunched over, he stayed low and stayed in cover. He was on the move, and now he had two soon-to-be dead men to track.

Chapter 10

Don't Look Back

Walking as fast as they could, Vin and Ethan were making quick time trying to get off the mountains. Vin was keeping a close eye on everything in front of them, while Ethan paid attention to everything that was to the sides and behind them. About every ten minutes while they were walking, he would turn around fully to make sure nothing suspicious was following.

They reached the crossing point of the stream, and the water still raged right to the top of the rocks. The log they had crossed swayed back and forth with the force of the water hitting against it. "I tell you what, this looks like it is going to be fun for us," Ethan said.

"Yeah, just a blast. Let's hear some ideas on how to get across without going under. What have you got?" Vin said.

"We have to get secured somehow. If we just chance it, all it will take is one slip," Ethan replied.

Taking off their packs, they rummage through them, looking for anything that could help. "Got it! I knew I remembered this," Vin said, as he pulled a roll of five fifty cord out of the bottom of his bag. "You thinking what I'm thinking?" Vin asked.

"Yeah, tie us off to either end, then use the other person and a tree to secure things just in case of a fall into the water," Ethan said.

"Exactly. Help me out here. I'll go first," Vin said, wrapping the rope around his waist and preparing to cross.

"Hold on a second," Ethan said. Running underneath a tree, Ethan came back with a long stick. "Hopefully this will help secure your footing."

"Well, hopefully it won't hinder me either," Vin replied sarcastically as he walked for the crossing.

Ethan wrapped the rope around his waist and proceeded to back around a tree, making sure to give himself as much leverage as he possibly could.

"You got me?" Vin asked.

"Roger that," Ethan replied with a thumbs-up.

Taking two deep breaths, Vin stepped onto the log, pressing the stick into the water next to him as he began to walk. The water beat against the log, wiggling it underneath his feet. With every step, Ethan released more slack. Ethan knew a pull at the wrong moment could cause Vin to slip just as easy as the wet condition of the log or rocks.

Reaching out in front of him, Vin placed the stick as he moved from the log to the first rock. Leaning forward, he jumped, landing on the rock, but his momentum continued forward. Vin managed to keep his feet under him, but the weight from his pack pushed his upper body forward. Just as he moved the stick in front of himself, he felt a slight pull at his back. Ethan had the rope tight, holding him right on balance. Vin let out one of the biggest exhales of his life. He continued to look forward as he lifted his right hand and shot Ethan a thumbs up. Now it would just be a balancing act from here. The rocks were all close enough, so he wouldn't need to make any more big leaps. *It's just one foot in front of the other,* he repeated to himself.

Using the stick to keep his balance, Vin moved slowly, but eventually made his way to the other side of the stream. "Hell, that was easy!" Vin shouted back to Ethan as he swung his hand to signal for Ethan to go next.

Barely able to make out what Vin had said, Ethan shouted, "Good to know there is nothing to worry about." He adjusted the rope and held up a thumbs-up to Vin signaling he was ready to begin.

They moved most of the rope to Vin's side so he could manage the safety net for Ethan. Taking his time, Ethan found a stick for himself and stepped onto the log, preparing to cross. The log still shook under the water pressure, so Ethan was meticulous in his movements. Coming to the end of the log, he prepared for the jump. "I hate this stuff. I'm short; I'm not a jumper," Ethan muttered to himself. With one leap, he landed right on the edge of the rock. A shot of what felt like electricity coursed up Ethan's spine as he barely managed to avoid falling into the water. "I hate that," Ethan muttered again.

Turning his attention forward, he began to walk again. The tops of the rocks felt as slick as ice, and with the water beating against them, he had to be sure of every step that he took.

"Looking good, keep coming!" Vin shouted.

Trying to maintain his focus, Ethan kept his head down as he moved forward. *Almost there, just four more rocks,* Ethan told himself. As he stepped to another rock, his stick found a sink hole on the water. His side immediately dropped out from under him, followed quickly by his footing. Ethan slid off the rocks, splashing into the water.

Vin tried to catch him with the rope, but the current mixed with Ethan's weight pulled him forward, slamming him into the tree he was wrapped against. The rope burned into Vin's hips as he held his ground. Every muscle in his body was tensed up, but he didn't let the rope slip even one more inch. Turning his head, Vin looked to see Ethan in the middle of the water doing everything he could to keep his head up. Gritting his teeth, Vin bared down. "Pull, come on, pull," he yelled. He took one step back. "Do it, damn it, pull!" Another two steps back.

Vin closed his eyes as he began to shake. He gained more ground now, taking another five steps back. Turning his head to look, Vin could see that Ethan was almost to the bank. Digging his feet deep in the mud now, Vin was having an easier time walking back. Ethan flailed his arms around him as water smacked him in the face. Vin continued to step back, and Ethan reached forward, slapping his hand on the bank.

"Well shit, if you wanted to go for a swim, why didn't you just say so?" Vin said.

"You know me, I always like to keep you guessing," Ethan laughed. Ethan extended out his hand as Vin reached down to pull him up. As he did though, a chill shot down his spine like a streak of lighting. Vin quickly pulled Ethan to his feet. Neither one said a word as they looked around.

"You have that feeling too?" Vin asked.

"Oh yeah, I do. You feel like we're being watched too?" Ethan replied.

"Big time. Let's just hope it's our minds just playing tricks on us." Vin began to wrap the rope back up. "Let's get this back together quickly. We need to get back to that outcropping and get a fire going to dry you off. I don't want you going hypothermic on us," Vin said.

Ethan looked right back at Vin, "Yeah, I'm freezing," he said.

Back on the other side of the stream, hidden low in the brush, Flint crawled across the forest floor. He didn't make a sound as he slid through the mud, keeping every movement methodical. He stayed low; his rifle was lying in his arms. Stopping just on the other side of the stream inside the brush, he lay his rifle out in front of him taking up a prone position. Trying to stay hidden underneath the brush, Flint cleared a spot in front of him just enough so that he could see through his scope. Peering through it, he began to steady himself.

The hunters were both standing broad side to him. The cross hairs in the scope were beginning to settle on the rib cage of the short, sopping wet man, though Flint couldn't get a steady rest on his rifle. His resting arm was too shaky. He shifted his front arm and flattened out his body even more. His aim was settling in as he slowed his breathing. The shaking was going away. Tightening his grip on the rifle, he moved his finger over the trigger, applying weight to it and, taking up the slack.

"Let's get out of here, I don't want to stay any longer than we have to," the taller of the two men said.

The short one took a step backwards, turning around, and they both began to walk back into the woods. Flint released pressure on the trigger, took his finger off it, and lifted his head. He half smiled and jumped to his feet, back in pursuit of the two men.

"We have to hurry and get back. I have to get a fire going. That water was freezing" Ethan said between chattering teeth.

"We're almost back to the outcrop. Once we get there, we will get that fire going ASAP. We just have to keep pushing," Vin said.

"I'm trying to, but with it getting closer to dark, I can feel my body starting to want to shiver. To be honest, you're not anymore dry than I am," Ethan said.

"For sure. I've been checking on the GPS, and if we keep this pace, I bet we are there within fifteen to twenty minutes, max," Vin said pushing straight for their camping spot from the night before. Once they realized how close they were, they both began to push the pace. After everything that had taken place so far, they both needed a place out of the rain.

They had around two hours of daylight left by the time they had finally reached the spot. First thing they did was go through their gear and grab some emergency fire starter, but there were only a few dry sticks left over from the fire last night. "Can you go grab so more wood?" Ethan asked.

"Can do," Vin replied as he shot out of the outcrop.

Ethan began working with the wood left there and started building a small fire.

Vin moved as quickly as he could to bring back extra firewood. By the time Vin returned, Ethan had a small but warm fire going. "Get ready, this will get pretty smokey here in a second," Vin said.

"So what you're telling me is that there wasn't much for dry wood out there?" Ethan said with a laugh.

"Oh, it was out there, but I just didn't feel like grabbing that stuff. I figured it would make things just too easy," Vin said.

"No, we sure wouldn't want anything like that," Ethan replied. "Well sit your ass down and get yourself dried off."

Meanwhile, Flint slowly crawled into the spot that he had marked from when he had visited the camp earlier in the day, sliding up next to the base of a tree and lying prone with his rifle rested on a root. He peered down into the camp through the scope. He could see the shadows that both men cast from the light; the light from the fire was the only thing that broke the blackness of the night. The storm still raged on around Flint. Even with how enraged the storm had become, due to living in the mountains for the last twenty years, Flint had turned into an instinctive and primal being. Living in the extremes was just another part of his life.

With how in touch he had become with the environment around him, Flint knew that the storm was about to take a turn for the worse. With the light from the fire, there was no missing the men. It would have been easy to shoot them right then, but there was a rock blocking his shot. As long as they were sitting down, he was blocked. Flattening out his body and steadying himself best he could, Flint made himself comfortable. The trap was set. Now it was just a waiting game to see which man would stand up first.

Both Vin and Ethan had pulled some food from their packs and now found themselves just trying to rest by the fire as they ate. "Can you believe we found that?" Ethan asked.

Vin set down his food. "Truly, I don't know what to think. I mean, I've seen movies about this stuff or occasionally you hear stories about a crazy guy in the woods, but nothing like this," Vin said.

"For sure. This is the stuff that your mind plays games about in the dark," Ethan replied.

"Let's just get our food down followed by a few hours of rest, then we hustle our asses out of here," Vin said.

They quickly finished their meals. Ethan put some more wood on the fire, building it back up then, scooted back against the wall of the outcrop. Right away, he tilted his head back, closing his eyes.

As Vin finished eating, he found a dry spot in the outcrop and positioned his pack at one end of it, then he laid down to get some rest. Unable to quiet his mind, Vin began to look around the camp. He looked around the entrance to the outcrop, then down at the ground; that's when something caught his eye. "Hey, Ethan, let me see the bottom of your boots," Vin said.

"Um, why?" Ethan asked.

"Because that track over there. You see it? I know that wasn't made from my boots," Vin said.

Ethan turned his head to see what Vin was talking about. His eyes widened, and every bit of air left his lungs. "Those aren't from my boots either," Ethan replied. Ethan turned back to Vin in complete disbelief.

"Someone has been in our camp," Vin whispered.

"Someone? Who the hell else would it be? It's the crazy bastard that lives in that cabin," Ethan said.

"Alright, we have a major problem now that we know we aren't alone. We can't wait any longer to get out of here. Grab your stuff and let's get moving," Vin said. They both grabbed their backpacks and began loading all their gear back up as fast as they could.

Resting next to tree, Flint once again let a smile grow across his face. The shadows were moving now, and he could tell with the speed that they were moving that one of them would expose himself soon. He steadied the rifle, making sure he had the best rest he could, closed one eye, slowed his breathing, and moved his finger onto the trigger. *It won't be long now*, he thought to himself.

"You have all your stuff loaded up?" Vin asked.

"Yes, you?" Ethan replied.

"Yeah, let's get going and get some ground covered in the dark. With this storm covering any light from the sky, I'm hoping that helps keep at least a few odds in our favor," Vin said.

Ethan turned and looked up to the sky. *This is going to be a rough exit*, he thought to himself. The sky was black as coal. The rain continued to beat down on the ground. Just as Ethan began to close his bag, he heard the first rumble of thunder off in the distance.

Vin began to rise to his feet, hauling his pack with him. He swung one of the straps over his left shoulder then turned to grab the other strap, pulling it over his right. He reached across his waist to fasten the buckle.

Crack! A rifle shot broke the air, and Vin was thrown off his feet and into the side of the outcrop.

Ethan dove to the ground, mud and the water splashing up around him. Turning his back to the rock they were sitting behind, Ethan looked back to see what had happened to Vin. "Vin! Vin!" Ethan yelled out.

Chapter 11

Being Pursued

Vin began to move, trying to push himself to his feet, not realizing what had happened.

"Get your ass back on the ground!" Ethan shouted. A mixed feeling of emotions fell over Ethan. He was relieved that Vin was back up and moving, but panic was starting to creep in knowing that they had been found.

Vin froze on the ground trying to gather himself. Shifting his pack off him, he crawled over to Ethan, dragging his bag and making sure to stay flat on the ground.

"Are you hit anywhere?" Ethan asked.

"Doesn't feel like it," Vin replied.

They stared at each other confused. If Vin hadn't been shot, then what threw him off his feet? Vin pulled his pack right up next to them, and that's when Ethan saw it. The bullet had just barely missed Vin and struck the metal frame on his backpack. They looked at each other wide eyes, unable to believe the near miss.

"Well, that's about as close as it gets," Vin said.

"Yeah, but now that we know this psycho has found us. Do you have any ideas for what we should do? I'm all ears for ideas," Ethan said.

Vin scooped up a handful of mud, throwing it on top of the fire, putting it out right away.

"That solved one big part of the problem," Ethan whispered.

Trying to think, they both laid in the mud under the cover of the rock hoping that with the cover and the fire now being extinguished that the man had lost sight of them. The last thing that either of them wanted was to give him another shot. Sitting in place, all they could do was hide.

Every heartbeat felt like it was shaking the earth. It felt as if time stood still. It was the slowest and the coldest passing of time either of them had experienced. There were no sounds of movement. All that they could hear was the sound of the rain hitting the rocks and puddles; nothing in the woods moved.

"Alright, at this point in the dark, I'm sure he doesn't have another shot," Vin whispered so quietly that Ethan was barely able to hear him.

"Agreed, otherwise he would have taken it," Ethan whispered back.

"With conditions being completely dark, I'm more worried about this guy trying to move in on us."

Vin could barely make out Ethan nodding in agreement. They pulled out their rifles.

"Keep your gun ready. If he comes around the corner, one of us will have to put him down quick," Ethan murmured.

"We are just going to have to take our chances in the dark. Let's break for the forest and just gun it right back to the other camp," Vin said.

"Then, I say we don't stop, but just grab the big packs and head right back over the mountain."

"If he doesn't close the distance between where he's hiding and watching us from, then I say we just wait till dark and make a run for the forest."

"Exactly, then just go for the truck, covering as much ground as we can." Ethan said.

Vin began to inch his way around the side of the rock. There was another rumble in the distance, but it was closer this time. "Well, now we get to run out of here in a thunderstorm, this just gets better and better, wouldn't you say?" Vin said sarcastically.

Ethan smirked, shaking his head. "Ease around that corner and let's get going," Ethan replied.

Vin rose to one knee and took a deep breath, closing his eyes. *It's now or* never, Vin told himself. As he exhaled, he rose to his feet, sprinting into the darkness and heading for the trees. Right behind him, Ethan rose out of the mud, doing the same. Once in the darkness of the forest, they could barely see anything, and neither one of them was about to turn on one of their lights. From here on out their journey was going to be in the dark.

Thunder cracked again in the distance, but this time it was followed by a quick strike of lightning. They ventured farther into the darkness, ahead of the storm. Behind them, the forest lit up with the quick strike of lightening.

When the forest beamed with light for that quick second, it was just close enough to see that there was nothing on the forest floor. No one was resting next to the base of the tree anymore. Flint had gone and was now moving through the forest under the cover of darkness as well.

Vin led the way through the trees as they traveled in complete darkness; neither man could even see his hand in front of his face. Every time they tried to run, they either ran into a tree or tripped over rocks and roots. As they tried to push the pace, most of the time they had to hold their hands in front of themselves. Even though they were trying to move as fast as they could, the thunder and lightning were quickly catching them. The lightening became bittersweet. Each strike lit up the sky and the forest, and for just a second it would let them see the world they were in, but it also gave Flint a chance to see them.

"Do you think this guy is watching us?" Ethan muttered.

"I'm not sure what is going on, but with what happened back at camp, I'm betting that wherever we go, this guy will be ten steps ahead of us. We're on his mountains, and with him now after us, I think the better question is how long has this guy been watching us," Vin replied. A strike of lightning lit up the entire sky. They were surrounded by trees.

"Hey, grab something to cover me. We should stop and get a heading before we get completely lost," Ethan said.

Vin pulled off his jacket and threw it over to Ethan to hide the light from the GPS.

Ethan pulled up the map with the trail they had hiked in on. "Shit!" Ethan wanted to yell, but it turned into a restrained whisper as he spoke.

"What's going on?" Vin asked.

"We're off course. Way off course."

"In the dark, navigating while trying not to show ourselves is going to be hard as hell," Vin said.

"What else are we going to do? We have to give it a try," Ethan said.

Pushing further on in the dark, Vin continued to lead the way through the trees. The lightning was all but on top of them now.

Another bolt struck down and the whole world around them lit up. Vin immediately stopped in his tracks. "Shit," Vin let out under his breath.

Ethan walked up to Vin's side. The next bolt of lightning came down, and Ethan could see it clearly now too. They were standing just inside the trees before the meadow that drops back down to the cliff lake area. "I wasn't expecting to show up right here," Ethan said.

"We can go farther down this side, but eventually we'll just hit the rocky side of that mountain. Then we'd just have to cross the meadow there instead," Vin said. Lightning cracked across the sky, lighting up the meadow once more.

"We're just going to have to cross it here, aren't we?" Ethan asked.

"Yup. We're going to have to sprint across the meadow to get to those trees on the other side, then we can use them to get down the side of the mountain with at least some cover," Vin answered.

"With this lightning lighting up the sky, there will be multiple times while each of us is running when we'll not only be out in the open, but completely visible," Ethan said. "I know we could try crawling or staying low, but honestly I want to be in that meadow for as short of a time as possible." Vin said.

Ethan thought for a few seconds thinking about what Vin had just said. "I agree. I know that with a run across we'll be exposed, but crawling we'll be out there for way too long, and if he's around. . . . Let's get out of there as fast as we can." Ethan said.

"I hate to ask the question, but do you think he is watching us?" Vin asked.

"Honestly, I have to wonder how in the hell he would be able to track us through this storm in complete darkness. At least I would think his tracking would be at a crawl. He has to be drastically behind us," Ethan said.

Both men took cover behind the trunk of the trees with the storm raging around them. The wind was howling, causing the rain to blow in from the side, beating down on them. The rain ran off the men like it did the trees and the rocks. Neither one of them wanted to cross that meadow, but it was the only way that they could see to get down the mountain.

"I'll go first," Vin said

"You sure? You went first out from behind the rock. I think it should be my turn to be the Guinea pig," Ethan replied.

"No, I will go first. Cover me, and when I'm about three quarters of the way over, you start. When I get in the trees, I'll turn around to cover you. Let's make sure to watch each other as closely as we can. We're going to have to be extremely careful," Vin said.

Ethan nodded his head, acknowledging the plan.

Static electricity filled the air around them. The hairs on Ethan's neck stood on end as his beard hair began to slowly lift. The hair sticking out of Vin's hat lifted as well. Ethan turned to Vin, "What in the . . ." Just then, a bolt of lightning came crashing down from the sky with an eruption of thunder not even a second behind it. The light temporarily blinded them, and the thunder was loud enough that the earth shook as they both covered their ears. The lightning had struck a tree a few hundred yards behind them. The tree exploded from the top down, sending fiery chunks of wood everywhere. As soon as the rumble stopped Vin looked at Ethan, "Now I sure as hell don't want to stay here."

Ethan gathered himself. "Here? Out there we'll be the tallest objects. Think that's any safer? We're just in a damned if we do, damned if we don't situation," Ethan said. The infuriated storm engulfed everything around them. Looking up, the sky danced with electricity. Behind them, they saw the leftovers of the burning tree. And ahead of them, they would be left completely exposed. Vin turned to Ethan, and Ethan could see fear on his face knowing what he was about to do.

"Well, here we go," Vin said.

That's when time slowed for Ethan. Vin moved his rifle off his shoulder and down into his hands. His knuckles turned white from the intensity if his grip. Lightning cracked again, seeming to cause the whole world to light up. Just then, Vin turned his head and took off at a dead run. The flash was gone, and darkness covered everything once more.

"Get there, get there. Come on," Ethan muttered to himself as he sat with his rifle braced against a tree. He didn't know what was out there, but he had to be ready for anything. With the next strike, Ethan could see him. Vin was halfway across, still in full stride. Ethan could see that the wind and the rain was beating against Vin and that he was doing everything he could to stay on his feet. Then the light was gone, and darkness fell again.

On the others side of the meadow, an eye leaned out from behind a tree. A low smile grew on Flint's face as he tilted his head down, looking out from under his eyebrows. He was waiting for them. His rifle was slung across his back, and he turned his head to look down at his left hand in which he held a tomahawk with a razor-sharp edge. He turned back towards the meadow, tightening his grip on the tomahawk. His next trap was set. The sky lit up and he could see the first man running toward him. In just a few more seconds he would have one less man to worry about.

The mud and water splashed around Vin as he sprinted through the soaking wet meadow. Multiple times he just about slipped as his feet caught slick spots in the mud. Vin was almost across the meadow, so Ethan should have himself readied. Vin was within ten yards of the trees, still in a full sprint and with no intention of slowing down. A bolt of lightning lit up the sky, and a man stepped out from behind the tree just in front of Vin. Vin could see a sadistic smile lighting up the man's face as a tomahawk rose behind his head. *It's a trap, it's a god damn trap. He's waiting for us,* Vin thought to himself as his heart sank. Vin tried to stop by shifting his weight, but his feet slipped out from under him and he began to fall backward. As he fell, the man drove the tomahawk forward, swinging right at his throat. The swing just barely missed Vin's face as he hit the ground flat on his back.

By the time Vin was about halfway across the meadow, Ethan had his gun in his hands and at the ready. He pulled the gun tight to his chest, closing his eyes. *It's just a few hundred yards. No problem. It's just another run, no big deal. I've got this,* Ethan told himself. He took off in a full sprint behind Vin. Lightening flashed, and Ethan saw Vin reach the edge of the meadow just as a man stepped out from behind a tree, swinging for him as Vin hit the ground. Letting out a giant gasp of air, a jolt of panic shot through his entire body. Ethan couldn't stop or turn around. He lowered his head, pushing himself faster than he ever had before. His steps became uncontrollable in the mud, but he didn't care. He had to push farther and faster. With the random flashes of light followed by complete darkness, Ethan knew he would never get an accurate shot. With the force that Ethan was pushing his legs now, they had become numb, and he couldn't feel the ground beneath his feet. His right foot stomped into the mud in front of him, and as he pushed off to continue forward, his foot slipped. He fell forward, landing flat on his face and sliding forward, pushing the mud in front of him.

Lying flat on his back, Vin looked up as another flash lit up the sky. Flint was laughing as he stood over him, pulling his arm back once more. Vin could see the light gleam off the tomahawk, just as the man began to drive it down with full force.

Vin rolled right as the man drove the tomahawk down toward his chest. The swing missed, sinking the tomahawk deep in the mud. As he rolled out of the way, Vin hit a patch of mud and started to slide again, bringing him close to the edge of the mountain. The mud slick continued down the steep side of the mountain, sending Vin over the edge. He smacked his head into the first tree, knocking himself out. Vin's Body went completely limp and he fell like a rag doll through the trees and down the mountainside.

Ethan pushed himself up to his knees, sitting on his heels, he grabbed his rifle, resting it on his knees as he looked up to assess the scene before him. Rain beat down, running off the brim of his hat. Another bolt lit up the sky, and he could see the man picking up the tomahawk from the ground. Vin was nowhere to be seen.

Everything went dark, and Ethan began to fumble with his rifle. Bracing himself on a knee, he took aim for Flint knowing he couldn't miss his opportunity. Multiple strikes of lightning began to light up the sky. Ethan scanned the tree line with the crosshairs of his scope. The movement stopped as he settled dead center on Flint. Ethan saw Flint standing with a revolver aimed directly at him. The brother's story of the lost revolver at the gas pump ran through Ethan's mind, and he thought the gun might fit the description they had given. Quickly, Ethan began to apply pressure to the trigger of his rifle, readying himself for the bang of the rifle.

Another bolt of lightning crashed down at the exact same time that the loudest roar of thunder he had ever heard shook the earth around him. Ethan twitched as he finished pulling the trigger. The bullet missed clean, far over the top of Flint. Lowering the gun, Ethan quickly opened the bolt to try and chambered another round, but panic was setting in. Trying to manipulate the gun seemed almost impossible. He was scared. Visions began to race through his mind of when he and Vin learned to hunt with their fathers. His whole life flashed in front of his eyes before stopping in front of his gun safe. *Why in the hell didn't you give that to her before you left? Well, it doesn't matter now*, Ethan told himself. Looking up, the crack of the gun filled the air, and the flash of a muzzle so bright that it completely blinded him. But Ethan didn't have to see to feel the strike hit his body. Ethan spun with the impact. He hit the mud, the momentum from spinning around causing him to slide, and before he knew it, Ethan was slipping down the face of the mountain.

Chapter 12

What Just Happened?

Vin started to roll over as he cracked his eyes open. A sharp pain shot through his side with the movement. That's when he realized that he was wedged against a tree. He had slid halfway down the mountain through all the trees and his body felt as if he had hit every single one on his way down.

As he opened his eyes completely, he realized it was still dark, maybe just a few hours from sunrise. The rain had stopped, though there were still a few lingering clouds. *What happened, and where on the mountain am I?* Vin thought to himself. He began to sit up, but an incredible pain shot through his side again. It took all his energy to just sit up and lean against a tree. As soon as he had himself somewhat adjusted in front of the trunk of the tree, he let his body give out, going limp against it. Pain shot through his rib cage so blinding that he began to go faint. Once the pain settled, his mind started to wonder back to the last thing he could remember. He had been staring up, the rain pouring down as a flash of lightning broke coal black sky. All he could see was what looked like an insane mountain man driving a tomahawk straight for his head.

Vin looked back up the mountain towards the way he had fallen and remembered rolling down the side and away from that man. He began to check himself over more, needing to know what other injuries he might have. With how badly his side hurt, there was no doubt he had a few broken ribs. He ran his hand over his face and could feel dried blood from his nose; it was broken. His arms were covered in small cuts from dragging against rocks, trees, and ground. His neck and shoulders were extremely tender to touch. Though he couldn't see, he knew he was covered in bruises based on how tender his upper body was. When he touched his legs, he flinched right away as his hand touched his right leg. Putting even the slightest pressure there felt as if someone was driving a knife into his leg. He could move them, but it wasn't going to be easy. Just thinking about trying to get up and move almost brought a tear to his eye. *Well, I can't say I have been in a worse way. For damn sure this one has to take the cake*, Vin thought to himself.

    Then reality started to set in and he looked around. *Ethan, where is he? I'm stuck halfway down this stupid mountain. What happened to my friend?* Vin also realized all his gear and his gun were missing as well. *Shit, on the fall I lost all of my gear. There is a mad man chasing us around these stupid mountains, and I'm sitting here completely beaten to hell and totally defenseless. How in the hell am I supposed to be any good to anyone now?* Vin thought.

He looked around, this time examining his surroundings. *Well, this is one hell of a bad situation, I'm going to have to be smart and think here. There is no way I'm going to find Ethan so that we can both get the hell out of here if I panic. Its time stay calm and to get shit back under control.*

Vin prepared himself to stand. His mind was racing knowing this would be excruciatingly painful. He took one deep breath, his lungs filling with air causing pain to slowly creep its way up his rib cage. It felt as if someone was slowly driving a knife into his side. With a second breath, he couldn't quite fill up his lungs as the pain grew worse. "Ah, that hurt like a bitch. This sucks just trying to breath," Vin said out loud.

Closing his eyes, he knew exactly what was about to happened, and he began to ready himself again. First, he ran it through his mind, trying to mentally prepare. Then, Vin exhaled and quickly followed it with another huge deep breath. Pain shot through his entire chest. Vin pushed his hands into the ground, pushing his back against the tree; pain shot through his thighs and into his hips. His eyes slammed shut, and he squoze them as tight as he could as a slight tear began to run down his face. The pain was unbearable, and his eyes began to water continuously as he tried to slide his back up the trunk of the tree and get to his feet. It took everything his body had just to try and make it to his feet; he was already completely exhausted. "Okay, well that completely sucked, so I'm just going stay positive here and say that now the worst of this is over. From here on out, things are only going to get easier." Vin turned and looked up the mountain. "Yeah, the worst is over and it's all . . ."he paused, exhaling, "it's all up the mountain from here on out."

Closing his eyes, Vin knew that this first step was going to feel like someone was stabbing him in his leg with an axe. *Here goes nothing*, he thought, stepping out on his right leg. As his foot hit the ground, pain raced immediately from his foot right to his hip like a strike of lightning. It was so sensitive it felt as if every single nerve in his entire body was in his right leg. "AHHHHHH!" Vin screamed at the top of his lungs. He hurried and swung his left foot forward to try and catch his fall as he threw his hand out to catch himself on the closest tree. The pain was so blinding that his vision was blurring, and he was gritting his teeth together so hard that they felt as if they were going to shatter. His heart was racing so fast and hard that he could feel it was pounding against his broken ribs. *I'm not leaving Ethan out here alone to die,* was the only thought that he would let enter his mind.

Mustering all his might again, Vin braced himself for his next step. He looked up the mountain one more time, thinking to himself, *just like searching for a blood trail on a wounded animal. That's where I last saw Ethan, that's where I'm going to start my search.* Pushing himself off the tree, Vin leaned up on his feet. He shifted is weight so almost every ounce was on his left foot. Taking his first step forward, his right foot hit the ground. Pain shot through his body again. His hands made fists, his knuckles going white. Vin squoze his eyes shut as he tensed up his entire body. *Come on. If you're going to get the both of you out of this, then you're going to have to cowboy up and power through it. It's not going to get any easier,* Vin told himself.

Doing everything he could to power through the pain, he sucked in a huge gasp of air that felt like someone punched him right in his broken ribs. "AHHHHHH!" He couldn't help it anymore, he had to let out another massive yell. Beginning to walk forward, he tried to change the weight from his right foot to his left. Every time he placed weight back on his right leg, the pain felt as if it multiplied by a hundred-fold. All it took was a few steps before his leg gave out, causing him to fall to his right side, smacking the ground on his broken ribs. As he hit the ground, Vin let out a massive gasp. Pain started to pulse through his whole body. Every pulse of pain felt as if it matched with the beat of his heart. His body began to convulse as he coughed uncontrollably while he did everything he could to gasp for air.

Rolling to his back, Vin stared up at the sky. It wasn't much, but it was getting closer to sunup now. Slowly getting lighter, the sky turned from coal black to slightly gray before the yellow of the sun began creeping into the distant sky. *I can't stand on my own feet much less get to and help Ethan,* Vin thought to himself. Using his left arm, he placed it underneath himself, then rolled over to his stomach and crawled back to the base of the tree he had pushed off from. Propping himself up to sit against the base of the trunk, his head went limp, slamming back against the bark on the trunk. *Shit, I would think that should have hurt.* Though with how bad his leg and ribs hurt, the pain of his head almost didn't even register with him.

Vin was completely exhausted; every breath hurt. Just sitting there hurt. The pulsating pain continued to course through his body. *What the hell am I going to do?* Vin asked himself. He had nothing on him that he could use to help himself. He checked his pockets, trying to see if there was even anything that he had left on his person that might help him in the slightest way, but anything that he'd had in his pockets was either smashed or had fallen out. His breathing began to lighten, and his eyes were getting heavy. His mind began to push closer to unconsciousness, and he could feel his body wanting to give out and quit.

As Vin's mind was close to slipping into unconsciousness his surroundings began to change. It slowly began to feel as of the forest was becoming more alive. He could hear the wind lightly moving through the trees. The birds were starting the wake up. He closed his eyes and lowered his head. Only letting one thing enter his mind. *This is it? This is how I check out,* Vin thought.

It made him think back to a joke he had made to his mother-in-law earlier that year. She had been lecturing Vin and Kasey for not having kids yet. Vin had responded with, "You will get grandkids from Kasey's second husband, after she remarries because I went missing on some Himalayan sheep hunt." He and Kasey had found the joke funny, but as soon as he'd said it, his mother-in-law shot him a look that could kill. She obviously hadn't agreed. It also hadn't helped that once Vin saw the look on her face, he had begun to laugh knowing that he had just intentionally made her completely furious. Remembering this exchange made him laugh, which was followed by pain in his ribs. *Well, I may have gotten the location wrong, but I guess I wasn't far off,* he thought.

He picked his head back up, cracking his eyes open. That's when he noticed it. He went from hearing every little movement and noise in the whole forest to not hearing a thing. The forest stood completely still, as if it was almost froze in time. There wasn't a sound, and an ice-cold chill froze Vin's spine. A new cloud had moved overhead, completely hiding the sun. The darkness settled around him. No birds and no wind whistled through the trees anymore. Then he heard a sound break the silence. Breathing in and out with a few very deep breaths, Vin closed his eyes. Not even having to open them, he knew something bad was about to happen and that there was nothing he was going to be able to do about it.

He's found me. Vin opened his eyes, looking to his left and seeing the same sight he had seen a few hours before. There he was, that same man that tried to take his head off. He still had that same crazed look in his eye. With his head tilted down, the man was looking out from under his brow with an insane smile painted across his face. Flint was slowly walking toward Vin, but it was like the man wasn't even there—he didn't make a single sound. He had an old worn backpack but carried a brand-new custom-made rifle. *Shit, I wonder where he got that*, Vin thought to himself. The closer Flint got, the more Vin knew this was going to be the last thing he would ever see.

Closing his eyes, Vin's life flashed before him. It raced like a movie on fast forward before coming to an abrupt stop and continuing in slow motion. He could see his wedding. He was looking straight in Kasey's eyes. His pulse slowed, and his body relaxed. *I fought for all that I had, but I can't push anymore this time. I don't want to give up, but at this point I honestly don't know what to do now. The next guy had better take damn good care of her.* Then his mind paused. *I was truly blessed to call her my wife*, Vin thought to himself.

It didn't take long before Flint was standing over Vin, just staring at him with that smile. Vin lifted his head up and opened his eyes. He stared right back at Flint. That was when he knew it: there was almost no life in Flint's eyes. There were no signs of compassion or remorse or even humanity left in him. All Vin could see was pure evil. He felt as if he was staring the devil himself right in the face. Flint raised his arms, and with one swing, the butt of the rifle smacked Vin a crossed the face. Then the whole world went black.

Flint stood over Vin's completely unconscious body staring down at Vin's face. Looking up, Flint turned his head and looked around examining his surroundings. Making sure no one was around him. Reaching into his bag, he pulled out a roll of duct tape. "I'll worry about cleaning up the dead one I shot later. First, though, I need to make this one disappear," Flint said.

Chapter 13

Starting at the Bottom

The sun had risen high and was starting to beat down on the mountains. The weather had cleared off, and the rays of sunlight broke through the trees as Ethan began to open his eyes. Sitting up, he slowly began to look around, trying to gain recognition of what had happened. He found himself in a valley at the bottom of the mountain. Turning his head, he looked back up, noticing that he had fallen uncontrollably down the clearing with trees on one side and rocks on the other. *How in the hell was I able to manage that one?* Ethan asked himself.

He had a massive headache, the pain behind his eyes almost blinding. Ethan began to look himself over, trying to find anything visibly wrong. His legs looked fine—a tear or two on his pants, but that was it. He made sure to wiggle his toes and move his legs to make sure that everything worked. Continuing to test his motor skills, he moved his entire body. Picking up his left arm, he clamped his eyes shut tight and clenched his fists. *Okay, that hurt like a bitch. What in the hell happened there?* Ethan said. He turned his head to look as he brought his right arm over to examine his left. At the top of his arm, just below his shoulder, he saw a gash that had ripped through the outer flesh of his arm. *Was this from the fall? No, it's from. . .*

His mind began to turn, and as he thought back, the night before flashed into his mind. A vision of rain pouring down in front of him. Flashes of lightening briefly lighting up the pitch-black sky. Through a flash, he saw the man standing in the tree line with a gun. *It was aimed directly on me. That was the last flash I saw. I was shot. I was shot and thrown down a damn mountain. All of that, and I'm sitting here with one small flesh wound and a few bumps and bruises? Someone had to be looking out for me on that one. I'm one lucky son of a bitch,* Ethan thought. As he began to regain himself, more memories from the day before began to rush back to him. As well as who else he was forgetting about.

Ethan remembered that in one of the lightning flashes he had seen the man swing a tomahawk at Vin's head. Then the flash of the muzzle of the gun ignited the world, and after that everything went to black. Once he realized all of this, his mind started to race. The realization was setting in fast: he and Vin had become separated. *Where is Vin? I have to get help for him. I have to find him; he's in trouble.*

Getting to his feet, Ethan began to analyze his situation. Looking around, he found his pack about ten yards up the mountainside. Relief filled his body at the sight of it. "Holy hell, that's as lucky as it gets," Ethan said as he started to walk towards the pack.

As soon as he reached it, he started to shuffle through the pack to get to his first aid kit. He began to disinfect and wrap a bandage around his wound. It was a very primitive dressing, but he just needed something that was going to get him through. He wanted to save as much of the kit as he could, not knowing what he might have to use the rest for.

Ethan continued to dig through the pack, he had to see what gear he had to work with. First thing he pulled out was his broken GPS. "Well, now knowing all the trails and the exact places of everything can just go out the damn window," he said. Shuffling through the rest of the gear, Ethan found that all his optics—spotting scope, binoculars, range finder—were completely busted. The only thing that wasn't broken was one small monocular. *Well, that won't help me much, but in a pinch, it might come in handy.* The small tool kit he kept for his rifle was still intact. There was a bit of food left, and his water filter and emergency fire starting kit were undamaged. Looking at that, a huge sigh of relief hit him. The camera he had used to take the pictures of the cabin was completely busted, but he made sure to take the memory card out of it. "Just in case," Ethan muttered to himself.

Digging farther into the pack, his hand touched a glass bottle.

Pulling it out, Ethan looked at the small bottle of 10th Mountain Whiskey. "How in the hell did that not break? I'll take that, as its not time yet," Ethan said. Next, he pulled out a box of ammo for his rifle. The outside was completely caved in, but he opened it hoping that maybe the damage had only been done to the box. Pulling out each round, he looked them over one at a time. The first few were bent, and a few more were smashed, but the last six rounds in the box were still good. He slid them into his pocket. As he finished looking, he let out a sigh of relief as he grabbed the map out of the bottom of the pack along with a compass that still worked. "Well thank you for a plan B," Ethan said.

Reloading his pack, Ethan began to plan. He started by looking at what he did know. He was at least a day and a half hike away from the truck. Getting to phone service would be almost two days away. He could try for it, but that's a long hike with a crazy man that knows the area like the back of his hand hunting him. Another option was to head down to the lakes with major people activity and maybe hope that he could run into other hunters. Then perhaps one of them would have a satellite phone he could use to get a hold of the police and search and rescue. Though that would still be a little over a day's hike.

All that Ethan could think to himself now was, *With the time it would take to get to help, then for the help to get in here and find Vin, well, by that time anything could happen, and I doubt that Vin, wherever he is, would still be alive. If he is now.* Ethan stood there running his hand across his face trying to decide what to do. He looked down at his leg, thinking of all the scars that covered his shin. That's when it ran through his head: he knew what Vin would do. Then his mind stopped again. No, he knew what Vin had done. Ethan threw the pack on his back and turned, heading back up the mountain.

    He looked around trying to get a path in his mind of where to begin. Looking straight up, Ethan saw the clearing that he had slid down. To his left at the top were the trees they had run out of to cross the clearing. Below those trees was a rock face. So, he peered over to the trees they had been trying to sprint to so they could make it down the mountain in cover. *I know Vin fell through the trees, so I'm going to need to go that way to find him,* Ethan thought. He took a few steps heading in that direction before he stopped and looked back at the marks he had made falling. He reached in his pocket and felt the six rounds he had placed there. *I'm going to need to see if I can find my gun real quick. With a mad man trying to hunt us down, I will need to have it back.* Starting back up the mountain, Ethan followed the exact path he had made coming down. It was slow moving. The ground had dried on top, but underneath was still slick mud. With every step up, Ethan had to make sure his footing was secure.

Around a third of the way up, he saw it. A rush of relief flooded Ethan's body. His rifle was sitting against a pile of mud. Rushing over to the gun, he grabbed it and began to wipe the mud away. He pulled out the magazine and checked to make sure the ammo was fine. Then opened the chamber and checked to make sure nothing had gotten in and plugged anything up. Throwing the gun to his shoulder, Ethan looked through the scope. "Okay, that sucks," he said. The glass was cracked, and the cross hairs were twisted. "Well, at least it has a lifetime warranty," Ethan laughed. Kneeling and taking off his pack, he pulled out the small tool kit. He quickly began to remove the scope. Luckily, when he'd had the rifle built, he also had iron sights installed. It just took a few minutes before he had the scope removed and the rifle was ready to be used with the other sights. "Never thought this would be why I would be switching these out, but sometimes things get a little western," Ethan said. After he switched out the sights, Ethan slung the rifle over his shoulder and headed into the trees.

Ethan moved back down to the bottom of the trees, not knowing how far down Vin had fallen. Even though he wanted to just race through the trees and back up the mountain, Ethan knew that he couldn't be in a hurry. He didn't want to miss anything, so he made sure to go slow. This was going to be just like tracking a wounded animal. It was going to take time, and he would have to pay attention to every single detail. Checking behind all the trees and trying to get the widest view that he could, Ethan kept moving up the mountain. He found nothing, not even a deer or an Elk track. It felt as if the entire forest had completely emptied. He looked up in the trees and all around him—nothing. The only thing alive in the forest was him. It took some time, but as he began to near three quarters of the way up the mountain, Ethan could see a spot that looked like something or someone had fallen in the mud. It was his first sign, and this is where the trail would begin.

Ethan rushed over to the spot, examining the mark on the ground. It was obviously the end of a slide. He turned his head and looked back up the mountain. He could see it: a clear slide coming down the mountain due to the mud. Ethan could see every skid, every roll, everything about the trail was clear. It ended with the slide against the trunk of the tree right in front of Ethan. Ethan knew that this had to be the tail that Vin made sliding down the mountain, but there was no Vin. Taking a deep breath in, Ethan closed his eyes. *Okay, obviously he was here. Next question, did he leave on his own?* The possible situations began to run through his mind, and his pulse began to race. *Stay calm. You can't help anyone if you can't control yourself. I found where he was, now I just need to make the next step in the puzzle. Exactly like tracking a wounded animal. There is a trail, just follow it,* Ethan told himself.

He looked around, first examining the tree and noticing some bark was rubbed off just in front of the mud slide. Looking at the ground, he also noticed that Vin's hands and feet had dug into the mud. *This must be where Vin pushed himself up against the trunk to get to his feet.*

Looking forward, Ethan could see the footsteps where Vin had begun to step forward to start back up the hill. Following how the feet moved, Ethan could see a few quick steps then what looked like a quick fall into the closest tree in front of him. A little higher up on the tree, he could see where something hit against it. It looked as if Vin had been unable to walk for long before his strength gave out. There were two spots on each side of the tree where what looked like two hands had peeled off some of the bark.

Vin is hurt bad, Ethan thought. He followed the movement of the feet, seeing how Vin pushed himself off the tree and then made his way around the trunk, still trying to move forward up the mountain. Watching the movement Ethan could see that the steps didn't go far. Ethan saw a few more quick steps then another fall mark in the mud. No, not just a fall, this one was a fall followed by a crawl. The crawl marks went right back to the other side of the tree. Then the marks of his hands and feet digging into the mud again so he could prop himself back up against the trunk. Raising his eyebrows and turning his head, Ethan was confused. These aren't the tracks of someone that could have gotten off this mountain. If this were a wounded deer or elk trail, this is where he would be expecting to find the animal. Because he had been so focused on the trail Vin had made, it took him a few minutes of searching for what he saw next to register.

There was another set of tracks walking right up to the trunk of the tree. Ethan turned to examine the tracks on the way to the tree, they followed the slide marks coming down the mountain perfectly, keeping a few rows of trees over. Examining the tracks after they lead to the front of the tree, Ethan saw that they turned and began back up the mountain.

Ethan took his hand, rubbing it across his mouth and down through his facial hair. Then dropped down to a knee seeing a difference in the tracks coming to and from the tree. That's when he realized it: the tracks leaving sunk into the mud more. "Damn it . . . this has to be the worst-case scenario," Ethan quietly said to himself with a sigh. The difference in the tracks signaled that Flint had been weighed down more when he left than when he had come.

Chapter 14

On the Trail

Glimpses of light and dark were flashing before him, and his head waved back and forth over and over. Arms and legs were dangling, his hands were bound with duct tape and he was hanging almost as if he were completely lifeless. As more light filled his eyes, he noticed the ground was moving below him, his head swung down, and his chin smacked against a shoulder. It jarred him awake more, and Vin realized that he was slung over the shoulder of Flint. That's when Vin noticed it: this man carried a backpack, a rifle, and a man over his shoulder and he was still walking fast and showing no sign of slowing down. Flint wasn't missing a step.

Vin looked around. They were climbing a mountain, and it felt as if this man was almost gaining speed. That's when it started to come back to Vin. Everything from the storm, waking up in the trees, and then Flint swinging the rifle at his head. Turning his head and squeezing his eyes, Vin felt as if someone was punching him in the face, the area pulsing with each heartbeat. Finally, what was happening began to register. Flint was hauling him off somewhere.

Vin had fully come to and began to do what he could to assess the situation. *I have to do something,* he thought. *I don't know if this will work, but it's going to be worth a shot.* Squeezing his hands to together Vin raised his arms. He swung straight down, driving with every bit of strength his body had into Flint's kidney. As a streak of pain shot through Flint's body, his right shoulder shot down as his back and chest went forward. He dropped Vin on the ground as he fell flat onto his back.

Vin landed right onto his ribs, letting all the air out of his body in a whoosh and leaving him gasping. It took a few moments, but Vin was finally able to get some air back into his lungs. The first sight he saw of the mountain and the trees went white. For a few seconds, he couldn't see anything; the pain was so intense it overwhelmed his entire body. Vin tried clutched his side as the blinding light left his eyes, and he could see Flint lying on his back next to him. *This could be my only chance. I have to do what I can,* Vin thought to himself.

His heart started to race uncontrollably, feeling like it was a fist trying to punch its way out of his chest. He rolled onto his chest, getting both of his arms under himself, and pushing up to a knee, leveraging to push off onto his right leg. His foot hit the ground, and he began to push down while putting the weight of his body forward. Vin could see the trees. His mind could only think one thing, get *in there and disappear from this guy. Get space between you and him.* He pushed himself up onto his right leg, "AHHHHHH!" His scream filled the air, and Vin dropped to his right side as his leg immediately gave out. It felt as if he got shot in the hip. Rolling to his back, Vin couldn't believe he had forgotten that his leg was hurt.

His arms pulled right back into his chest as his body was completely overtaken with pain. His eyes cracked open as his head rolled to the left. Flint was moving slowly, rolling over to a side to begin to stand up. *I have to move; I have to do something. I can't just lay here,* Vin thought. He raised his hands to his mouth and began to rip through the tape with his teeth. Once his hands were free. He rolled back over to his stomach, his body filled with adrenaline to mask the pain. His head was down, but he peered out from under his brow. *Get into the woods. Disappear! Go! Go now!* Vin screamed in his mind.

Once again, he tried to run for the tree line, throwing his right leg forward. The pain overshadowed everything. The air raced out of his lungs, and Vin's chest smacked into the ground again. Turning his head to look over his shoulder, he saw that the man had reached his feet and was picking up the gun from the ground.

I can't quit. Keep fighting. I will do what I have to! He is not going to kill me with my own gun, Vin thought. Turning forward, Vin saw a rock on the ground in front of him. He rolled his left arm underneath himself, curling his left leg in. His right arm stretched out in front of him, and with one painful motion he pushed and pulled, diving forward. Vin's right hand landed on the rock. Pulling it into himself and rolling to his back, Vin placed the rock in both hands above his head. Flint was turning around, holding the rifle low in both hands. Vin saw his face, there it was that sadistic smile again, looking out of the top of his eyes. Flint was enjoying every minute of this fight.

It was now or never. Vin hurled the rock at Flint with every bit of strength his body could muster. A shot of air exploded out of Flint's lungs. The rock smacked him in the chest, and the gun fell to the ground. Vin's first move was to go for it, but Flint dropped to his hands and knees with his body covering the weapon. "Damn it!" Vin shouted. Rolling back to his chest Vin pressed himself up onto his hands and his left leg.

Whatever it takes, just go! Vin screamed to himself. Staying on three limbs, Vin jumped on his left leg, then threw his hands forward, dragging his right leg. He moved forward, but the pain from his ribs shot through his chest when his arms hit the ground. He couldn't care about the pain now, this could be his only chance. He continued to jump forward as fast as he could physically push his body. *Don't look back till he catches you or you get to the tree line,* the thought raced through his mind. There was no sound except for his heart pounding against his rib cage. *Thump, thump, thump,* it raced through his mind.

As he reached the tree line, Vin vaulted his entire body forward into the bush at the base of a trunk. He smacked the ground; it took every fiber in his body to keep himself from screaming out in pain. He knew that being injured he would leave a huge trail, but this was the chance he was given to try and get away, so he was going to have to do anything he could to take advantage of it. Rolling back, Vin saw that the man had the rifle back in his hands and was slowly getting back to his feet. That sadistic look hadn't even wavered, in fact it looked like it had only deepened. That's when Vin realized that the hunt had turned into more of a fight, and that had amped Flint up even more.

Flint rose to his feet and started to stalk toward the trees where Vin was hiding. Vin rolled over and began to crawl, paying attention to every move he made and trying to be careful. The slightest sound would be sure to give away his position. He stayed as flat as possible, just trying to hide in the underbrush and listen for Flint, but he wasn't making a single sound. Not a twig broke under a single step. Not even the sound of his pants moving as he walked. *Who can be that quiet?* Vin's mind raced. *Stay low and stay quiet. Whatever you do, you can't panic. You have to keep your head no matter what happens or you are truly screwed,* Vin thought to himself.

Vin crawled into the thickest part of the underbrush he could find. *Unless he steps on me, he will never see me here. Just stay down and don't move*, Vin repeated to himself. Lying there, he could barely see behind him, but that was good, it meant that his cover was thick if he could barely see Flint. And Flint would have a hard time finding Vin as well.

Flint entered the brush with still not a sound. He moved and turned his body in ways that the brush didn't even touch him. Vin lay there waiting and waiting for sounds of Flint to walk past him, but he heard nothing. He had no idea where Flint was now. Vin's heart began to race, knowing that Flint had to be getting closer. Closing his eyes, he lay there like he was frozen in ice, not moving a muscle. Vin even tried his best to keep his breathing to a minimum. All it would take was the slightest noise or movement and his position would be given away.

Flint walked towards the area he last saw the hunter, not making one sound. His pants didn't even drag on the brush as he stepped forward. Every time he set a foot down, he placed it slowly, and he would slowly roll his foot off twigs, preventing the weight of his body from breaking them. He passed farther through the brush, not taking long before arriving at the spot he last saw the man.

Swinging his head back and forth, Flint began to examine the ground for the first indication on where to start looking for a trail to follow. He knelt to one knee, slowly turning to look across the ground. It didn't take long before the right side of his mouth grew, bringing the return of the sadistic look to his face once again. Dropping his right hand to the ground and sliding it forward, it wasn't hard for him to tell this was where the crawl marks started. Standing back up, he lowered his body so he was hunched over, just like a cougar stalking its pray. He was back on the hunt.

Vin's hands clenched tight; his knuckles were ghost white from squeezing. He took a deep breath in and held his eyes shut, feeling like they were sewn closed. He held his breath, terrified to let it out in fear of showing any form of movement. Blood rushed to his face, and his lungs felt as if they were going to burst from his chest. He held that breath for what felt like an eternity. *Don't move, don't you dare make one single movement. He's going to walk right passed you. It will be better to pass out then have him find you. You know how that will end.* Vin kept repeating the words in his head. He felt as if he were about to pass out, and when he began to let his breath out, he exhaled through his nose as slowly as he could release the air from his lungs. Once at the end of the breath, Vin slowly opened his eyes and saw him.

Flint raced forward, pulling his leg back and putting all his strength into his swing forward, kicking Vin as hard as he could right in the stomach. The force of the blow rolled Vin farther into the brush. Vin continued to roll, making it to his stomach and trying to crawl away with every muscle in his body. He didn't get far before a second swing came, Flint's boot smashing into Vin's broken ribs.

"AHHHHHH!" Vin screamed out in pain as he curled himself up into a ball. Flint smirked again, swinging the rifle off his shoulder and down into both of his hands. Holding the rifle low at his waist, he aimed the muzzle right at Vin's chest. Turning his head, Vin looked down at the muzzle of the rifle settled a few inches from his chest.

His racing mind slowed, and his pulse began to calm. Vin was coming to terms with what was about to happen. *Is he going to shoot me this time?* Curled up in pain, all Vin could think to himself was, *well maybe if he shoots me, it will be the easiest way out at this point.* The tension in his muscles began to relax. "Go ahead, just shoot me. You're just going to kill me eventually, so why wait?" Vin said.

Holding Vin's own rifle on him, the man just stood there staring at him, not saying a word. No emotion crossed his face. His finger slowly moved off the trigger, and he clicked the gun back onto safe.

Vin watched as he did this. His heart began to race once again, *Shit, he's not going to kill me yet*, Vin thought. Flint turned the gun again, the muzzle aiming straight up in the sky. He swung the butt of the rifle right into Vin's ribs again. Vin wanted to scream, but he couldn't even muster that. The pain engulfed every inch of his body. His eyes began to twitch closed and water. He had never experienced this level of pain in his life. Vin had been pushed to his physical and metal limit for the first time, and he was breaking down. Rolling over onto his back, he looked straight up. The man walked closer now, standing directly over his body as his legs straddled Vin's chest. He saw Flint raising the rifle once more. *One more time*, Vin said to himself. Flint drove the butt of the rifle down again. Right at Vin's head. Once again, the last thing Vin saw was that sadistic smile.

Chapter 15

Tracking

Ethan had begun following the trail that Flint had left. He quickly made his way back to the top of the hill; the tracks had headed straight up next to the trees. Ethan could tell Flint had taken the path of least resistance. Now that he had all this extra weight to carry, he'd had to slow down his movement, but the rest of his trail would not be that easy to follow. The tracks turned and headed into the forest right where Ethan had last seen Flint. It was right where Flint had been standing when he'd shot at Ethan. Knowing this insane man had taken his friend, all Ethan could think was that he had to catch him as fast as he could. He knew racing through the forest blindly was a terrible idea seeing as there was no way he could know what was around the next corner or chance losing the trail. And Ethan could not lose this trail. Every second counted right now.

Holding his rifle at the ready, Ethan followed the tracks from the edge of the clearing, then he turned and rounded into the first trees. Stopping to check the trail, Ethan dropped down to one knee. He hung the rifle in his left hand as he looked to check the direction of movement. That's when he noticed something he had missed before:

there were drops of blood between the steps. Not only were there footprints, but now there was a blood trail. The last thing he'd wanted to come across was a blood trail.

The tracks went deep into the trees. He was now traveling in the complete opposite direction from their camp. It was a slow process, though it eventually led Ethan to the stream. He was farther downstream, just past the meadow where he and Vin had found the Elk. The stream had slowed from the storm and the slope had flattened out some, causing the current to slow down. There was chest high grass that had grown on the banks. Ethan looked down, trying to examine the tracks. He could tell the man had stopped here to take what was probably a small break. The tracks turned to look upstream for a few steps before turning and heading down it. Following them down to a few of the trees, he rounded a tree following the tracks. That's when Ethan saw Flint's point of rest. Looking around, he could tell where Flint had set Vin down and where he had sat at the base of a tree.

There was some blood that had gathered on the ground in the spot where Vin had been set. Continuing to look around, Ethan picked up the movement of the tracks again; they walked right into the stream. With the water slowing down, the stream wasn't terribly deep or fast anymore. He didn't want to get his feet wet, but Ethan needed to hurry, so he didn't have a choice. Stepping forward, he entered the water, wading to the other side of the bank now with from his thighs down completely drenched. Luckily, the sun had come out, and the temperature had risen. *I sure hope that decision doesn't bite me in the ass later*, Ethan thought. Following the tracks, he pushed deep into the thick trees, while also turning at a slight angle and heading for the base of the higher mountains.

Ethan's tracking slowed down again. Following the trail in this extremely thick underbrush was difficult, and the blood trail wasn't heavy enough anymore to spot it in this brush. *Shit, I would have thought he would have made one hell of a trail in this brush. I mean, he is carrying another person for hell's sake. This guy moves like a damn ghost sometimes,* Ethan said to himself. It took some time, but he stayed on the trail and eventually came out of the thicket and into a small meadow where the tracks where a lot easier to find. Even though he was walking through the meadow, Ethan noticed the trail turned and skimmed the edge of it. He noticed that the entire time Flint made a point to be able to get himself out of sight easily.

Halfway around the meadow, Ethan stopped when the tracks went from walking to what looked like a big disturbance. The grass around the area was flattened, like Flint had dropped Vin. Ethan slung his rifle over his shoulder and knelt to examine the ground closer. It looked as if two bodies fell on the ground. He could see how one body had tried to move then fell back to the ground, smashing every piece of grass as it moved. He knew this one had to have been Vin. "The crazy son of a bitch was finally able to fight back," Ethan said.

Looking around, he could see the spot where Flint had landed. Ethan could see how he made it back to his feet. His tracks followed right in the direction that Vin had moved. Ethan could see that Vin was doing some sort of a makeshift bear crawl. "He must have messed his leg up bad, but he's got the will to live. That guy will fight to the end, no matter what has happened," Ethan said.

He could see exactly where Vin dove into the brush, getting out of the meadow. Then continued finding where Vin rolled into the undergrowth and hid. "He wasn't giving up for nothing," Ethan said. Turing around, he examined the ground more closely, and the second set of tracks began to come into view. Ethan could see these were from Flint. They moved right on top of the tracks Vin had made. "Good hell, is this guy a damn blood hound? Not missing anything, he walked right along the same trail Vin made and right up to where he was hiding," Ethan said. Looking around, noticing a spot where it looked as if there was another struggle.

Ethan knelt and reached his hand down, touching the ground. There was a little bit of blood that had run onto a rock. Ethan ran one finger over the blood spot. It went right onto his finger; it was still wet. "Well, I'm not as far behind as I was, I'm gaining ground now. That's the good news, but now Vin is in worse shape than he was before. I'm going to have to kick things in the ass even more," Ethan said.

Standing back up, Ethan unslung his rifle. He opened the bolt and pushed around in the chamber. Knowing that he was gaining some serious ground, Ethan knew anything could change at any moment, and he needed to be ready for all the possibilities. Turning around, Ethan saw that the tracks started moving again, but along with that there was a slight blood trail with them once more. Ethan was back on the trail, pushing into the forest. He stayed right on the trail they were making footprints along with the blood trail. Ethan was gaining speed. The trail continued to run deeper towards the base of the mountains. *Where in the hell is he going? This is a long way from his cabin. And from what I can remember from his maps, Flint doesn't have any hideouts down this way either. What is this guy thinking?* Ethan thought as he walked.

He kept following the trail, stopping to check it on a regular basis, looking for any changes or for any more signs of a struggle, but no such luck. The blood was no longer fresh now, what little he could find was drying up. "I sure as hell hope this doesn't mean I'm falling farther behind. I have to speed this up," Ethan said.

Stopping, he knelt to look at the footprints. Then he turned his head to his right, and that's when he saw it. *Shit!* There were more tracks on the ground—they were paw prints. "That's what he's doing.

There is a mountain lion den down here somewhere. He's going to use it to get rid of a body. These paw prints aren't fresh, though with the scent of fresh blood in the air this close to a den, it may not take long. I can't afford to fall behind now. I have to catch them," Ethan said.

He was closing in on the base of the cliffs, and the forest was still as thick as it ever was or could be. Ethan had to push his way between pine tree branches. A few times, the branches whipped back causing pine needles to stick into the back of his neck. Ethan cringed every time. *How in the hell does this guy get through this shit at full speed?* Ethan asked himself. He looked up, trying to catch a glimpse of the sky. He was in the shadow of the mountain now. The sky had all but disappeared, and the stone wall of the top of the mountain was now almost all that he could see. The forest dove deep into what was turning into a canyon. With the rock walls closing in around him, he had to move as slow as he possible could. Any sounds that he made would echo through the canyon. Then Flint would immediately know that he was being followed. Taking his eyes from the sky, Ethan knew it wouldn't be long until this trail came to an end. Then he would be at the base of the mountain.

Ethan dropped low, hunching over and trying to quietly move forward. He held his gun in his hands; with no idea what lie just ahead of him, he wanted to make sure he was ready for whatever it maybe. His heart was beating hard, feeling as if someone were swinging a sledgehammer from inside his chest trying to get out. Sweat was running down under his hat, pouring off his head. *For all I know, this guy has a trap waiting for me right around the next corner. Or that mountain lion could come up on all this, too,* Ethan's mind raced. Stopping at the base of a tree, Ethan pressed himself flat against the trunk and slowly peered around the side. He squinted, trying to see through the tree branches and brush, but as hard as he tried, Ethan could only see maybe twenty or thirty yards at best.

Ethan dropped down to his knees and began to crawl. He stayed low and moved slowly, the closer he got, the more things began to come into his view. The thirty yards he could see extend another thirty yards, and then another. Stopping where he was, Ethan saw something. It was movement right on the edge of his view. He wasn't able to make out much of what was going on, but he could see what looked like one person moving around what looked like a limp body. Ethan continued to crawl forward. He drew closer and closer; his gun rested across his arms as he dropped once again and began crawling on his belly. His fingers dug into the dirt as he moved. Ethan was within fifteen yards of the tree line. Crawling up to the base of a tree,
Ethan slid up to one knee and peered around the trunk. He could see Flint had laid Vin against a pile of rocks, his head hanging low and limp. Ethan looked closer and saw that Vin's feet and hands were

bound. A sigh of relief quietly left Ethan's lungs; there was no reason to tie up a dead man.

There were low hanging branches on the tree he was hiding behind; Ethan could see Flint, but he needed to move to be able to lift the rifle and get a clean shot. *This could be my only chance. I have to figure out a better position. I can't screw this up,* Ethan thought. Flint was moving something around and adjusting Vin's body. Ethan tried to slowly swing around the tree and get in position for the shot. Moving his rifle up and off to the side of the tree, Ethan was almost ready. There were still a few branches in his way. He pushed his body even lower. *I can't risk the bullet hitting a limb*, Ethan thought. As he finished moving into position, one of the branches scratched against his backpack. The sound broke through the silence just like a gun shot. Flint's head shot around, looking right in the direction of where Ethan was kneeling. The look sent an ice-cold chill right down Ethan's spine. Flint hadn't even had to look around for where the sound originated; he had just known exactly where it had come from. *One sound, that's all it took and he immediately knew right where I am,* Ethan thought. Ethan threw the safety off on his rifle and took aim, but Flint had disappeared once again.

Chapter 16

Don't Move

Ethan looked around in every direction, but Flint had vanished into thin air. *What in the hell do I do now?* Ethan thought. Turning his head back toward Vin, Ethan began to move forward first, going for his knife to cut Vin's hands and feet free. He walked forward hunched over holding his rifle in his left hand and field knife in his right. Just before exiting the tree line, Ethan froze in his tracks. He turned his head up, trying to see whatever he could be on the cliffs above, then he turned to his left and right. *Shit, I can't just walk out into the clearing. He's probably waiting for me to do just that. Then he'll kill two birds with one stone,* Ethan thought. Slowly putting his knife away, he slid back into the trees, making sure to keep himself in cover. A rock slid off one of the cliffs, and Ethan shifted his head to his right. *He's watching me. I knew it.* Backing slowly farther and farther into the trees, he tried to watch the cliff lines, but they were disappearing fast behind the trees.

He's going to be back on the ground soon now that I have backed into the forest. I have no idea where he is, and I bet he is just waiting for me to somehow leave myself exposed. I must stay in as much cover as I can, the thoughts ran through Ethan's head as his heart pounded, his hands shook, and sweat still poured off his head. Ethan pushed into the thickest cover he could find, dropping down to his stomach and crawling along the ground. He moved at a snail's pace, trying to keep himself from making any sort of sound. He had already seen what happened when he made a sound before.

A twig broke twenty yards ahead and to his left. Trying not to jump at the noise, Ethan stopped moving and tried to pinpoint the sound; Ethan wasn't going to risk showing himself if he didn't know right where the man was. He waited silently, not moving, and doing his best to be completely invisible. He waited. Ten minutes passed by with nothing; not another sound was made. The entire forest was completely still. Then a rock rolled off something, making a loud thud as it hit the ground. A chill shot up Ethan's spine like lightening. This sound was to his right and behind him. Laying his head down, feeling like his heart was going to burst from his chest, Ethan held motionless. He knew he wouldn't be able to get the advantage.

Perhaps twenty minutes passed this time before a tree branch snapped directly to Ethan's left, maybe ten yards from him. If that far. Ethan's body wanted to react by rolling away to his right, but he stopped himself. It took everything he had to keep himself from reacting. *That's what he wants. He's toying with you, making noise on purpose, trying to let fear overtake your mind. He knows you're around here somewhere. If he can get you to snap, then you'll give yourself away. Just stay where you are and keep motionless and quiet. He's going to have to step on you to get you to move,* Ethan told himself over and over.

Ethan stayed there quietly, letting the time pass and hoping that the man had continued to push forward searching for him. About another hour had passed, and Ethan didn't hear another sound. His hands began to move, and his feet dug into the ground. He slowly crawled out from under the brush. With every inch he moved, he kept his head turned to the left, then to the right, moving his eyes and trying to see everything he could. He moved his rifle low and kept it in his hands at the ready. Hunched over, he stayed low watching every step he took. He moved to the left of where he had been hiding, going right for where the branch had broken.

Once there, Ethan dropped down, finding Flint's tracks, and began to follow the trail. They headed back toward the meadow where the struggle with Vin had happened, though taking a different route than Ethan had originally tracked him on. Flint was traveling parallel to a game trail; it was a rougher path that he had taken this time. It was thick, but still passable. *Why did he take this way? He must be trying to cut me off again like he did to us before,* Ethan thought. He moved silently, the only sound a light breeze whistling through the trees. It was getting later in the afternoon by now. In just a few hours it would start to get dark.

Trying to keep his head on a swivel, Ethan looked all around him keeping watch to his left and his right as well as in front. The tracks led to a small hill. He stopped and knelt next to a tree, trying to keep himself in cover. Looking at the ground he examined the tracks. Turning his head up he looked at the small hill; the tracks went right over the middle of it. It was about ten feet to the top. Ethan slowed his pace, trying to stay low. He didn't know what could be waiting for him on the other side. Taking his hand off the front of the gun, Ethan wiped it down the side of his pants, drying off the sweat. He proceeded to do the same with his other hand, making sure to get a good grip on the rifle.

Ethan reached the top of the small hill, looking at his surroundings he could see the meadow roughly fifty yards ahead of him. He scanned everything around him in all directions. Not one thing in the forest was out of place. He looked down to see the next step on the trail, but there were no more tracks. They had just disappeared; he had reached a dead end. *What in the hell? Tracks don't just end unless you've found what you're tracking. Feet don't just stop making footprints in the dirt,* Ethan thought. The wind stopped, and now there was nothing. Complete silence. The hair on his neck and arms stood straight up; the air almost felt electric. Ethan felt as if the entire world had stopped moving in that moment. Turning his head all around, looking for any cover, Ethan needed to find somewhere to hide. That's when the realization began to settle in: he was completely exposed and there was nowhere to hide now. It was a trap, and he had walked right into it.

Ethan kept turning, looking all around him. *I need to move. I need to hide. I have to get out of the open, but where is he. Which way do I go? Where is he waiting for me?* One more quick turn to his right and Ethan saw Flint. Everything moved in slow motion. Flint was stepping out from behind a tree, raising a rifle right at him. Trying to bring his rifle up in return, Ethan fumbled his footing while trying to gain control of himself and his feet slipped out from under him.

Flint was walking forward, gaining on Ethan as the rifle made its way to his shoulder. Flint closed one eye as he leveled the gun.

Ethan tumbled backward toward the edge of the hill.

Flint pulled the trigger, and the crack of a rifle broke the silence of the air.

Ethan's foot found the edge of the hill and he fell backward, tumbling down the small hill. He landed flat on his stomach. Every hair on his body was standing on end, and he could feel his fingers and toes tingling as his entire body surged with adrenaline.

He looked up the hill and could see Flint just about to crest the top. Ethan turned, finding his rifle lying next to him. He reached over with his left hand, grabbing the gun. Looking up, he saw

Flint chambering another round. Ethan turned, using one hand to push himself to his feet he began sprinted off into the trees.

As the second hunter disappeared into the trees, Flint stood at the top of the hill, lowering the rifle. He tilted his head down, looking out of the top of his eyes with his long greasy hair hanging to the sides of his face. A smile grew on his lips from under his untamed beard as he took his first step off the hill in pursuit.

His heart pounded, his lungs raced, and it felt like his feet were moving a thousand miles an hour. Ethan sprinted through the forest; tree branches smacked him in the face and he tripped over tree roots. *He's going to kill me, I know it. He's everywhere. This guy is outsmarting me every step of the way*, Ethan thought as he ran. He had sprinted past the meadow and was halfway back to the stream. He caught a root from a pine tree and fell flat on his face. He crawled up onto his hands and knees, then leaned himself against the trunk of the tree. He clutched the rifle tight against his chest, his heart still pounding, his eyes wide open, and his lungs completely drained of air. *What in the hell am I supposed to do now? This guy is inhuman. He tracked both Vin and I before, and all but killed us both. Then when I tried to track him down, all I did was make the slightest sound. That was it. My damn backpack just touched a tree branch, and he knew exactly where I was. Then he set a trap for me. How damn stupid did I have to be? I literally walked right into it, like a live animal trap.* Panic was racing through Ethan's mind.

Ethan was losing it; everything that had gone wrong kept replaying through his mind. *A trap, a stupid trap. It wasn't even anything elaborate,* Ethan thought. *Wait, wait just a second.* Ethan's eyes closed a little bit, his heart started to slow, and he began to catch his breath. The world had moved to slow motion. Then Ethan tilted his head down and a smile started to grow on his face. *A trap. He'd walked me right into one. All I did was follow him. He gave me the illusion that I was hunting him, that I was right on his trail. All he'd done was give me a false sense of control. But now I'm in the lead; now he's tracking me. He thinks he is tracking a panicked man that is completely lost in his own backyard. Well, now I'm going to have set my own trap.*

Turning his head up, the sky was getting dark. He slowly tilted his head back down. This was it; the descending darkness would give him a slight advantage over Flint. Once back on his feet, Ethan turned in the direction of the stream and began to pick up his pace again. He wanted as much time as he could to get his plan set up.

Slowing down his pace, Ethan stopped right on the bank of the stream. Looking to his right, he could see debris slowly flowing down from up the mountain. He stood a little farther down from where he had crossed earlier that day. Standing right in front of the flattest part of the stream, the long grass that had grown through it was waving in the slight breeze in front of him. The shadow of the trees overtook Ethan's location. Then he looked up at the sky and saw that the sun was beginning to set. "Okay, how am I going to set this thing? I've got to hurry, he'll be here soon. It won't take him long to follow that trail," Ethan murmured.

He led his trail right through the stream, making sure to go through the tall grass. There was no chance Flint could miss that he went this way. Once Ethan was on the other side of the stream, he checked around the area. He made a few quick steps in the dirt, wanting to make it look like he was in a panic. "That should give him a false sense of security," Ethan said.

Turning to his left, Ethan saw a small game trail that led through the brush alongside the stream. *That's going to be my ticket*, Ethan thought. Beginning down the trail, he looked for anything that would give him the advantage and found a small clearing fifty yards down. The game trail walked right into it. Stopping right in his tracks, Ethan surveyed the entire clearing; it was maybe twenty yards in diameter. It was a small feeding area. A little off to the side, but almost straight across from him, there was a downed tree. It was wedged next to another tree that was still standing right on the edge of the clearing. The smile returned to Ethan's face. *Right there, that's the perfect spot*, Ethan thought. As long as the man walks right down the path, he will be in the perfect spot

Ethan went straight across the clearing and took cover behind the downed tree. He stayed low, not knowing how far behind him

Flint was, and made sure to keep behind the cover of the tree trunk. Crawling to the end, Ethan made his way to the point where the downed tree met the one still standing. He leaned in tight to the trunk of the vertical tree while he swung his rifle up, resting it on the downed tree's trunk. The trap was set, and now all he had to do was wait for Flint to show up.

Ethan waited in position. It was getting late now, the sun having begun to hide behind the shadow of the peaks. It was getting dark. *He can't be that far off; this guy moves so damn fast,* Ethan thought. Tightening up on his rifle, Ethan made sure he was comfortable. He wasn't going to miss this chance, no matter what it took. It didn't take long before the sun had completely faded away. A cool air had settled over the mountain range. The breeze had stopped, and the sky looked like a sheet of reflective glass with a giant full moon shinning overhead. In the shadow of the trees, it was pitch black darkness. *Unless he has a spotlight, he's never going to see me,* Ethan thought. But in the clearing, or even anywhere the moon could make its way through the trees, he could easily see anything. It was almost just like daylight with a slight gray haze over casting it.

Ethan gripped his rifle tight, double checking that he had already loaded a round into the gun. Turning his head, he made sure that if he had to move, there would be nothing for his clothes to scratch on. Pacing himself now, Ethan made sure to get his breathing slowed. Calming down his heart rate, he had things lined up for the perfect shot. He wasn't going to let anything mess up his shot this time. This ended here and now. His ears listened for the slightest movement. Nothing broke the quite of the night. Ethan kept his eyes sharp, knowing they would be what saved him. Flint never made a noise unless he wanted to.

Shifting his eyes in front of him, Ethan scanned the area again and again, panning from right to left. Just as he was about to center his focus, he saw movement. Slightly off to his right, a shadow was moving. And there he was, walking right down the same path Ethan had come in on. Ethan gripped his rifle tight, fitting it into his shoulder. The shadow came closer down the trail. Ethan's heart rate picked up. He felt it racing and settled in his breath to get himself under control again. Flint got closer. He wasn't fifty yards away now. Ethan moved his finger slowly from the side of the rifle, settling it on the front of the trigger. Ethan positioned his head on the stock of the rifle. Settling his head, his eye came to rest right behind the rear sight. Ethan slowed his breathing once more and gained control of his body. In just a few seconds he would taking the shot that ended all of this, and the only trouble he would have left would be getting Vin and himself out alive.

The shadow came closer. Thirty yards. Then twenty. Ethan closed one of his eyes; Flint was one turn away from entering the clearing. Ethan could roughly tell where he was and he tried to get Flint in his sights, but the brush was too thick and he couldn't get a clear shot. Continuing to wait, Ethan slid his thumb up to the safety. Flint was just about to turn the corner and walk into the opening. Pushing the pressure forward, Ethan moved the gun out of the safe position. *Click.*

Flint stopped where he stood.

Ethan furrowed his eyebrows. *What in the hell is he doing? Come on, its only like six steps. Just take the damn steps! Come on, step into the damn opening! Do it already!* Ethan screamed in his mind. The shadow began to make slight movement, but the movement was backward. Flint was backing away from the clearing. A noise broke the silence of the night, it was a low and very deep laugh.

What in the hell was that? I didn't do anything to give myself away, Ethan thought. The shadow moved farther away, and the laugh was still the only noise breaking into the air. Before long, the shadow had disappeared into the darkest parts of forest. The only indication Ethan had of his location was by the laugh. Then it hit him. *Holy shit! It was the safety. That nearly inaudible click of the safety was all it took to for that man to know that I was waiting for him!* Ethan's eyes widened and about shot out from his head. If he heard the click of the safety going off, he now knows the general area that I'm hiding in. *Shit, shit, shit! He has the advantage now. I need to move again.* Ethan thought.

The laughing stopped, silence overtook the night again, and now Ethan had no idea where Flint had gone. *Okay, he's still tracking me. I can reset this trap. I just have to keep thinking,* Ethan told himself. He got up into a crouch. If he went into the clearing, he would be exposed right away. Thinking over the odds, Flint would probably come at him from roughly the same direction that Ethan had come himself. Ethan rounded the tree and began to head back toward the stream.

There wasn't any form of clearing in front of him. Ethan had completely engulfed himself in brush and trees. Trying to stay low, Ethan was doing everything he could to not only stay hidden, but to keep from making any form of sound as well. He had already been given away twice; it wasn't going to happen again. Ethan crawled along the ground, turning his heading back toward the stream. Checking over his shoulder, Ethan saw that Flint had made it to where Ethan had been waiting for him. Right where he had set his trap. *Shoot him. This is it; he's right in the open,* Ethan thought. Turning his head around, he grabbed his rifle and rolled over onto his side. He manipulated the rifle, turning it back around. Still lying on his back, Ethan tucked the gun into his shoulder and drew it up to aim, but Flint was gone.

What the hell? Where did he go? Think. He is hunting me, so what would be his next move? Rolling back to his stomach, Ethan began to crawl forward once more. Moving beneath the trees, he had only gone a few feet forward before stopping dead in his tracks. *He's hunting me. This guy tracked me this whole way,* Ethan thought. A smile covered his face, and he began to back up toward where he had set the trap. Standing back up, he checked the ground for more tracks. Flint had walked right up to where Ethan had begun to crawl, then he had stepped back, and the trail made its way back through the clearing. *That son of a bitch is headed to cut me off. If I had emerged from the thick trees by the stream, he would have been waiting for me. But I have the edge now,* Ethan thought.

Turning around, Ethan stepped around where he had hidden and skirted the edge of the clearing. Flint's tracks went right out in the open, he hadn't been worried about staying in cover because he had been in a hurry to get his trap set up. Ethan kept tight to the trees, making sure to conceal himself in their shadows. Anything could be a trap, and Ethan wasn't about to risk it. Following the trail, he quickly found his way back to the tree line.

He had to slow his movement to a crawl once he stepped into the trees, doing everything he could think of to keep a watch on his surroundings. If Flint were watching Ethan in hiding, this would be the spot to do it. Ethan held his rifle low and stepped lightly, keeping his movements smooth and ducking around each tree while making sure not to make one single sound. He took full advantage of following Flint's trail. Once Ethan reached the edge of the trees, he found himself on the bank of the stream. Posting up on the trunk of a tree and slowly peaking his head around the corner, Ethan got a visual of what he was about to step into. Flint was there, waiting for Ethan to crawl out from under the trees. He was kneeling with his rifle resting on a big rock on the edge of the stream. The barrel of the rifle was aimed directly at the trees. This was the moment Ethan had been waiting for, he had the edge on Flint. *You have the advantage now, don't screw it up*, Ethan told himself.

Ethan held his rifle straight up and leaned his back against the trunk of the tree. Tilting his head down, he took a deep breath. His heart was racing, and his hands were shaking. He took in another deep breath; his heart rate began to slow, though his hands continued to shake. For the second time in just a few hours, he was going to aim a rifle at a man. *Am I really about to shoot a man?* The thought raced through Ethan's head over and over. *I have to do this or else neither Vin nor I are going to get out of this alive. It's him or us*, Ethan told himself.

Moving his rifle into his shoulder, Ethan slowly began to swing around the trunk of the tree. He braced himself, kneeling at the base of the tree. Nothing made a sound. A round was already chambered, and his safety was off. Bracing his forearm on his knee, Ethan closed one eye and centered the other behind the rear sight. He took a deep breath in and then slowly released. His front sight settled, aiming right at Flint. He moved his finger from the side of the gun and settled it on the bow of the trigger. The front sight stayed right on Flint's bicep; from the side like this, this would be a center mass shot. He pulled the trigger.

Bang.

The shot of the rifle echoed through the silent mountains. The flash from the muzzle erupted in a blinding light. For a split second, the darkness became as if he were staring right into the sun. The light instantly blinded Ethan, but it was followed by a splash in the water.

Ethan ducked behind the tree, making sure to stay in cover while his sight returned. Slowly, he peaked his head around the trunk. Nothing. There was nothing there. He took a deep breath and opened the bolt on his rifle, ejecting the empty case, then pushed it forward, chambering a loaded round into the gun. He stepped out from behind the tree and got up to his feet, exposing himself in the moon light. He held the rifle low, but ready. Nothing was around. Flint had vanished again. Taking a quick glance up, the moon was at its highest and brightest point in the sky. The movement of the water running next to him broke the silence. His hands were as steady as a rock now, but every beat of his heart felt like a caged animal was trying to burst from his chest. Ethan was almost to the rock and there was no sign of Flint. No trail of his leaving.

He swung the rifle up, ready to aim and ready to shoot. Ethan began to circle the rock. *He could be lying in wait for me on the other side,* Ethan told himself. He turned to face Flint's hiding spot. There it was, a broken rifle lying on the ground. Stepping forward, he examined the side of the rock — blood coated it, the dirt, and the broken rifle laying on the ground. The metal of the gun was intact, but the stock was snapped in half. Kneeling, Ethan began to examine the tracks that had been left. He couldn't tell exactly what had happened, but he knew that Flint was now wounded. Ethan slung his rifle over his shoulder and studied everything closer. *From what I can tell, the bullet found this guy. While I had been trying to get my sight back, I'd heard a splash. I guess the impact of the bullet threw him into the stream. If he's dead in the water, my troubles are over. But if he's not dead, he'll at least be a hell of a way down stream and slowed down,* Ethan thought. Reaching over, he grabbed the front half of the broken gun, holding it as he stood up. He took off his pack and undid one of the straps, buckling the half of the rifle to the outside of his pack. *I'm not wasting anything we may need. It could come in handy.*

Chapter 17

The Journey Out

Covering ground as fast as he could, Ethan all but ran through the forest to make it back to Vin. Ethan was moving along the easiest trails that he could now and was almost always fully exposed in the moonlight. It still took some time, though. Checking his watch, he saw it was almost three a.m. now. Moving through the forest, Ethan knew he was getting close to where he'd left Vin. "Vin! Vin! You up there? Vin!" Ethan yelled.

"Ethan?!" Vin's voice echoed back through the trees.

"Yes, I'm on my way. Everything okay?" Ethan yelled back.

"No, no it's not! If it's not too much trouble, hurry your ass up!" Vin yelled back.

Moving to a full sprint, Ethan raced through the forest. Tree branches smacked him in the face, whipped him in the chest, and scrapped across his arms. This close, he couldn't let anything slow him down.

He broke through the trees at the back of the canyon. Vin was lying back against the base of the cliff with both hands and feet bound. His eyes were so wide that they were ready to burst out of his head.

"To your right! To your right! Look to your damn right!"

Ethan spun to his right side to find biggest mountain lion he had ever seen readying to leap off its feet right at him. In the next heartbeat, the lion was flying right toward him, its mouth opened as wide as it could. Its teeth were stained black in the moonlight from whatever else it had eaten earlier. Its front paws reached out in front of the it, exposing its razor-sharp mud- and blood-stained claws.

As the mountain lion lunged for him, Ethan began to fall backward, tripping over his own feet. He swung the rifle from his shoulder, getting it into both of his hands. He fired a quick shot from the hip and landed flat on his back. The mountain lion landed right on top of him, and the air exploded out of his lungs. Nothing moved. Ethan lay motionless, the mountain lion flat on top of him.

"Hey, hey, Ethan, you alive? Are you okay?" Vin asked, shock quivering his voice.

There was a long pause, then, "Well, I'm not going to lie, I have been better," Ethan said in agony. He shifted his weight to his right side and rolled the mountain lion off him. It rolled onto the ground, and Ethan slowly pushed himself to his feet, then bent down and grabbed his rifle. He poked the lion with the muzzle of the gun, checking for any signs of life. Rolling the animal over, Ethan saw an entry wound right in the heart of it.

"I'll give you my house if you can pull that one off again," Vin said with a laugh

"I think I'll just buy a damn lottery ticket on the way home," Ethan replied, shaking his head. Walking over to Vin, Ethan pulled out his knife and cut his hands and his feet free. Standing back up, Ethan undid the buckles on his pack and set it down, laying his rifle next to it. He pressed his back against the canyon wall and slid his feet out from under himself to sit on the ground next to Vin. "Well how was your day?" Ethan asked.

Both men burst out in laughter. "Oh, shit, don't make me laugh, it hurts like a son of a bitch. You know, when we go on an adventure and shit goes south, it really goes south," Vin replied.

"It's just like our dads always said, if you're going to do something, make sure you do it right."

Both Ethan and Vin rested their heads against the canyon wall, laughing hysterically. They slowly stopped laughing, and Vin turned serious, "Is Flint still out there?"

There was a short pause. "I will tell you all the details later, but I shot him. Now we just need to get out of here." Looking down at his watch, Ethan saw it was close to five a.m. "The sun should be up soon, so we'd better get some sleep," Ethan said. They both let out giant sighs. Each man had given every bit of energy they had to get to where they were now and neither one was about to move. They tilted their heads back against the canyon wall and closed their eyes, passing out from exhaustion.

Vin was the first to wake up, blinking at the sun that was now high above them. Turning to his left, he saw that Ethan was still sleeping. He swung his hand, hitting Ethan in the head. "Wake your ass up, we're burning daylight," Vin yelled.

Ethan jumped and rolled, crashing into his pack. "Good hell, dude, just give a guy a bit of a nudge," Ethan shot back as he pushed himself back up. Vin had started to laugh again as Ethan finished waking himself up. Once on his feet, Ethan stretched and looked at his watch. It was 11:18 a.m. "Okay, let's get this figured out before I start hauling your ass out of here. What do we have to work with? How beat to hell are you?" Ethan asked.

"Well, I have a smashed nose if you can't tell, and probably a few other broken facial bones," Vin said.

"Those are the least of my worries. What else we got going on?" Ethan asked again.

"Pretty sure I broke at least two ribs. I can breathe, it just hurts like a bitch," Vin answered.

"Alright, that's more what I'm worried about. What else?" Ethan asked.

"I'm not sure what it is, but I can't put any weight on my right leg; it just gives out every time. It hurts to move it, but I can. I just can't put weight on it. Other than that, just cuts, scraps, and beat to hell," Vin said.

"Okay. It's going to be a hell of a journey, but I can get you fixed up enough to get you out of here," Ethan replied.

First, Ethan had to find a way to tend to Vin's leg. Searching around, he soon found a sturdy stick just a little bit longer than Vin's leg. He placed the stick next to Vin, "You know what I'm doing right?" "Oh yeah," Vin answered.

Shuffling through his pack, Ethan pulled out the roll of five hundred fifty cord he had in the bottom and lined the stick up with Vin's leg, the top right at his hip and the bottom just past his foot. Ethan pulled out his knife, making a few notches in the stick where he was going to tie the cord to help prevent it from slipping around. He wrapped the cord first around Vin's hip.

"Come on, get that thing tight. If I'm going to have a peg leg, I don't want it falling off," Vin said.

With a sharp move, Ethan pulled the rope tight.

"Yup, yup, that's good," Vin said with a gasp.

Moving down his leg, Ethan finished securing Vin's new brace. Then headed back to his pack and pulled out the first aid kit. Searching through it for a minute, he soon pulled out horse tape.

"What are you going to do with that, wrap my feet like a horse, so I don't roll an ankle? Vin asked.

"If you don't keep your sarcastic comments to yourself for a bit, I could just leave your ass here," Ethan replied.

Vin shrugged, "Eh, that's fair."

Ethan walked over and quickly wrapped Vin's ribs, hoping to help secure the breaks a little bit. "It may not be insurance approved, but it's going to get the job done here. Now, let's figure out exactly where we are and get a plan to get out of here," Ethan said. Reopening his pack, Ethan pulled out the map and a compass.

"So, where are we?" Vin asked.

It took a few minutes for Ethan to find his bearing. "Alright, we are a good ways off course, but it is doable to get back, though it'll take a lot of extra time hauling you around," Ethan said.

"I don't mean to be such a burden, but come on, a psychopath did try to kill me," Vin replied.

"Milking it for all its worth," Ethan retorted as he studied the map closer and closer. Staring in deep thought, his right hand moved up and down the map, tracing new trails back and forth and making sure to examine all their options. "Alright, looks like the only real solution is to just stick to the original plan we had. If we tried for a new route out, we might only get halfway before we would both be toast. The quickest way out is our original route in, but there is no way in hell am I getting you even halfway out going that way," Ethan said. "Well, we aren't going to make it that far out today. So, what is our first play here?" Vin said.

"If we hustle the best we can and pray, then maybe tonight will be as clear as last night was. I think we can make it to our original base camp. So, let's keep our fingers crossed. I figure we can rest there for a while where there is shelter, extra food, and more medical supplies. We'll stop there for a few hours, then just move as fast as we can on whatever trail we choose after that," Ethan said.

"Sounds like a plan. Let's get the hell out of here," Vin said.

Ethan folded up the map and put everything back in his pack. Ethan grabbed one of the straps and swung it up on his back. He held his rifle in his left hand and extended his right to Vin. "Let's get the hell out of here," Ethan said.

Vin grabbed Ethan's hand, and Ethan pulled Vin to his feet. Slinging the rifle across his back, Ethan pulled Vin's right arm over his shoulder and propped Vin up to his feet, acting as a crutch for Vin.

They moved at a crawl, having to stop time after time to give Vin a chance to rest. Ethan was giving it everything he had to keep them moving at a steady pace. Though he didn't realize how bad of shape Vin was truly in, he knew that he had to keep pushing. Before long, they were able to reach the stream. Ethan leaned Vin up against a tree to keep him on his feet then began to search around. It didn't take long before Ethan found two long sticks. "Okay, put one of these in your left hand and I'll take the other in my right; they should help keep us stabilized. The last thing I need is for you to tip over in the middle of the water," Ethan said.

"Let's just get this over with, but when we get to the other side, I'm going to need a damn break," Vin replied.

"Rodger that," Ethan answered as he propped Vin up on his shoulder. They both knew they should avoid getting their clothes wet, but at this point they just went for it, slowly stepping into the water.

"Oh, shit that is cold," Vin said.

"Yeah, I had to cross it twice last night, so deal with it," Ethan replied. Pushing through the water, the current felt a lot stronger this time as Ethan battled to keep Vin on his feet.

Once they reached the middle and the water was at its deepest, every step Vin took felt as if the water was going to sweep his right leg out from under him. The only thing keeping him on his feet was Ethan taking the brunt of both the current and his weight every time he moved his leg. They battled their way across the stream, and Ethan struggled to drag Vin up on the bank. Making it up to dry ground, Vin was completely exhausted and barely had the strength to move. Ethan helped prop Vin up on a downed tree to try and catch his breath. Ethan dropped their gear and sat down on the ground.

"Well, that sure sucked," Ethan said.

"Agreed. So question. What in the hell happed? How did we end up here?" Vin asked.

"I only know my side of the story, what all do you remember?" Ethan asked.

"Right as I was trying to cross that meadow, that guy was waiting for me and tried to kill me. Then I fell down the mountain, hitting something on the way down, and got knocked out. Once I woke up, this guy found me as I was trying to get back up the mountain to try and find what had happened to you. He knocked me out again and basically kidnapped me. What happened with you?" Vin said.

"Well, he got a shot off at me," Ethan said, pointing at his shoulder. "Then I went sliding down the clearing of the mountain. I must have been knocked out by hitting something too. I eventually woke up down at the bottom around midmorning. I gathered as much gear as I could that was not broken and jumped on the trail that guy had left," Ethan said.

"Yeah, but how in the hell did I end up by a mountain lion den?" Vin asked.

"Once I caught up with him, I realized that is how he was going to get rid of your body. Just like all that other crap we found in his cabin," Ethan said.

"What happened to him? Why isn't he trying to run us down right now?" Vin asked.

Standing up, Ethan swung the pack back on and slung the rifle on his back. Then he grabbed Vin and pulled him to his feet. "I got a shot off. I know it hit him, so hopefully the only worry we will have now is to get our asses out of this damn place," Ethan said.

Meanwhile, there was movement a few miles downstream. Flint lay on the bank of the stream, half submerged, and face down in the dirt. Moving his head, he pressed his hands down into the mud, pushing his body up and dragging his legs out of the water. Rising to a knee, he pushed his long hair out of his face. His palm was covered in wet blood. He turned around to look at his reflection in the water. Blood was running down the side of his head, over the right side of his face, and down into his beard. He picked up his right arm where he had cuts from the jagged edges of a broken rifle stock.

Flint turned around, walking up onto the bank, and sat on a rock. He swung his old worn pack off his back and began digging through it. Pulling out a wrap, he began covering his wounds. After covering them up, he pulled out a map of his own. Laying it out, it wasn't long before he knew exactly where he was. Moving his hand across it, he came to the first spot he had circled, and his hand stopped. The words above it read "their spike camp." Then his hand moved down to an x above which the words read "ambush point."

Just down from the x was another circle by Cliff Lake, the caption above it read "their base camp." There were arrows marking the trail around the mountain back to the lake by the road. A circle with a line through it reading "their truck" was noted as well. Flint stood up as he put the map away. "I cannot let them get out of these mountains alive," he said.

Chapter 18

Making a Plan

The darkness of the night had engulfed the entire valley. Clouds had settled in, and the moon had almost disappeared. A small flickering light was making its way around Cliff Lake. Ethan had Vin's arm around his shoulders as he pulled him around the bank. "Good hell, I thought you would be a lot lighter than this," Ethan said.

There was a pause as Vin gathered the strength to come up with a reply. "So now you're calling me fat. Thanks jackass," Vin said sarcastically.

Both men were completely exhausted. It had taken every fiber of strength they each had to get Vin down that mountains safely, and now they were both running on empty. "Betting that tonight was going to be as clear as last night was the wrong choice," Vin said.

"It doesn't help now that my light is starting to die," Ethan replied. His head lamp continued to flicker.

"We're by the lake. We have to be getting closer now," Vin said.

They began to turn along the bank. Letting out a sigh of relief, they both knew their camp should be just a little farther in front of them. Ethan adjusted Vin on his shoulder and tried to pick up the pace. Ethan tilted his head up, looking ahead. His light flickered, but he still saw them. "We're there, man. Theres our tents," Ethan said.

Vin sighed and mustered all the strength he had left. Ethan pulled them both right to where they'd had the fire a few nights before. When they reached the side of the fire pit, both men collapsed to the ground. Vin rolled over onto his back.

With the pack and guns on his back, Ethan just lay face down on the ground.

"Okay, I'll just say it, maybe we shouldn't have gone for that extra little hike," Vin said.

Ethan burst out in laughter, causing dust to fly all around them. "I have no idea why, but damn that is funny." Ethan pushed himself to his knees and began taking everything off his back. "Stay there and try to rest. I'm going to get a fire going and get us some food."

Ethan gathered some wood, taking it back to the same spot where they'd had their first fire. He placed the wood in a tipi shape, stuffed some grass and leaves underneath it, and pulled his lighter from his pocket. He stopped to look at it, "I don't know how you didn't break when I fell down the mountain. God must have been watching out for us on that one."

Vin began to sit up, wincing in pain. "I have to say, I'm sure glad he's watching out cause I would sure hate to see him pissed off at us," Vin said.

Ethan shook his head as the small flames began to build up. "Get your hands up here and start getting warmed up," Ethan said.

Vin slid closer to the fire as Ethan stood and walked over to the tents. Unzipping one of the tents, he shown what light he had inside, and his eyes shot open wide. His fists began to clench, and he could feel his blood begin to boil inside of him. Ethan turned around, bent down, and snatched up the first rock he saw on the ground, throwing it as hard as he could right out into the middle of the lake. "Son of a bitch! I mean good hell, could we catch a damn break, or is that too much to ask? Damn it!" He bent down again and grabbed a large stick, throwing it through the air. The sound of it snapping echoed through the valley as it hit a tree.

Vin lowered his head, and he closed his eyes, "How bad is it?"

"That son of a bitch has been here too! All that is left are the damn tents, he looted everything. We don't have shit now. All that is left is whatever is in my bag," Ethan said.

Vin didn't know what to say. He remained silent as Ethan grabbed a few more sticks and walked over by the fire. "Sit down. Just sit down and throw a few more logs on the fire. Obviously, there isn't much else we can do now," he said.

Setting three more logs on the fire, Ethan sat down directly across from Vin. "This hole just keeps getting dug deeper and deeper.

No matter how hard we try, we just can't seem to gain any sort of ground," Ethan said. His voice was full of defeat.

Vin could see a look in his eyes. He could see that Ethan's mind was wanting to give up and let the doubt win. That was one thing he couldn't let happen. He knew Ethan had to keep his head up; there was no way either one was going to end this journey alive otherwise. "Look at me."

Ethan's head didn't move.

"Pick your damn head up and look at me, damn it!" Vin said.

Slowly, Ethan began to lift his head.

"Alright, do I have your attention?" Vin asked. Ethan didn't say a word, but he was looking Vin right in the eyes. "Good. Yeah, we're in a pretty shitty spot. But remember shit happens, and we have to deal with it," Vin said.

"How long was he following us? He's been ahead of us the entire time," Ethan replied.

"That doesn't matter! I don't give a damn. Look at how far we have come thanks to you! You have been keeping this shit together. You have been driving this forward. You even got the drop on that bastard, so don't you go giving up now. We have that pack and one and a half guns, so open that pack up and see what we have so we can plan for tomorrow," Vin said.

Ethan began to calm himself and turned to grab his pack. Opening the top pouch on the bag, he pulled out two smashed power bars. "We'll have to ration them, but they will help keep the edge off," Ethan said.

Vin snatched the bar out of Ethan's hand and immediately began to rip the wrapper open. "Holy shit, in circumstances like this, this is the best meal that a guy can eat," Vin said.

"After all that shit happening, anything in your stomach is the best meal you have ever eaten," Ethan said with a slight laugh.

As they ate the power bars, Ethan dug through his pack, pulling out the map and compass. "Well, let's check things out." Ethan said as he laid the map out next to the fire.

"Just considering the circumstances, we need to head for the main trail. It's going to be a bitch though, with you as banged up as you are. I'd say a positive estimate, if everything goes well, it will take us at least two days," Ethan said.

"Don't you think we should stay positive then?" Vin said.

"There's just one kicker, though," Ethan said.

"And what would that be?"

"Well, you see this hear?" Ethan pointed to a spot on the map where the trail had a sharp incline before it flattened out, then circled around a point of the mountains. "Making that ascent is going to be a royal bitch, and potentially dangerous, with me awkwardly carrying you," Ethan said.

"So, do you have a different idea for us, or are we going to just try it and give it hell?" Vin asked.

Ethan continued to examine the map for a moment, running his fingers down different trails, and looking at every single option they might have. "I have something. Though I doubt either one of us is going to like it," Ethan said.

"Well, that would be par for the course. Show me what you're thinking," Vin said.

"See where the incline starts on the trail? If we head for that, instead of going up, we can skirt around the bottom of the mountain. Now we will have to go back up eventually, but when we get around to the other side, it won't be near as sharp of an incline," Ethan said.

"That sounds great, but I feel there is a kicker to it that you haven't told me," Vin said.

"Yeah, that's the fun part. You see this section right here?" Ethan pointed to the map. Vin leaned forward and looked at where Ethan pointed. "That is a floating bog, an area where a lot of the streams flow into with poor drainage, basically forming a swamp," Ethan said.

"Shit. And if we go around that?"

"Then add at minimum another day and a half, if not two," Ethan replied.

"So, in all reality, we don't have any choice. We have to go for it," Vin said.

"Basically, yeah, that's our only option. So, get ready because tomorrow is going to be one hell of a bad day," Ethan said.

Vin laughed and laid back on the ground, "I sure hope it won't get worse than what we have already seen."

Ethan threw more wood on the fire, then laid on the ground across the fire from Vin. "With how this trip is going, it just might be. So, get some rest tonight because for all we know, these next two days could get really bad," Ethan said as he closed his eyes.

Both men settled off to sleep. Meanwhile, high up on top of the mountain, there was a slow and soft rustling of tree branches. Flint had made it to the top of the mountain and walked past the trees, stopping right at the edge. He dropped down to one knee, looking out over the valley below him. Everything in front of him was completely black. There wasn't even a star in the sky to light things up. No, there was one small glimmer of light. It came from the bottom of the valley. It seemed to be flickering and dancing; it was a flame. Flint smiled, nodding his head. Pulling his map out of one pocket and a very dim light out of the other, he took a few moments to examine it. He slowly folded the map and the light back up and placed both back in his pockets. Standing up, he adjusted his pack. He wore both the pistol and the tomahawk on his hips. Grabbing the tomahawk in his left hand, he held it up, staring at it. Once again, he began to smile. *Right where I thought they would be*, Flint said as he began walking deep into the forest once more.

Vin rolled over, slowly opening his eyes. A small bit of light had begun to settle on the valley. His first sight was of a smoldering pile of coals. Sitting up carefully, Vin looked over to see that Ethan wasn't sitting across from him anymore. Scanning his surroundings, he spotted Ethan at one of the small streams that ran into the lake. "Hey, you're not taking off and leaving me here, are you?" Vin shouted.

Ethan was filling up a water bottle from the stream. Twisting the cap back on, he leaned up and looked over his shoulder. "After all the shit that has gone on, I'm not going to lie, I probably should. You seem to have become more trouble than you are worth," Ethan said with a laugh. Standing up, Ethan placed the bottle in his pack and pulled out two more power bars. He walked over to Vin, handing him one of the bars. "It's not much, but it's all we have. Plus, we are going to have to really ration the last couple. Who knows when we will get more food?" Ethan said.

"Hopefully, it's only going to be about a day and a half before both of us are in a hospital getting fixed up," Vin replied. Ethan extended his hand, Vin grabbed it, and Ethan pulled him to his feet. "Well incase things do end up going that way, do you still have it in the pack?" Vin asked.

Ethan smirked and reached into the pack, pulling out the bottle of 10th Mountain Whiskey.

"Well shit, not even a crack on it," Vin said.

"Yeah, I'm not sure if that's a good omen or a bad one," Ethan said.

"Either way, I'm keeping a prayer in my heart that this is going to be one more trip where we still won't have to crack the seal on that," Vin said.

"Just give it a few days and I'll have it back on the shelf in my house," Ethan said as he placed the bottle back in his pack. Swinging his pack onto his back, Ethan clipped the front buckle and slung the rifle over his shoulder.

Vin swung his arm around Ethan's shoulder and propped a stick under his arm for his crutch. Vin turned to look at Ethan, "Let's give it hell."

Ethan didn't say a word, he just nodded his head and began to walk forward.

The sun had reached the top of the sky. It was midday, and Flint had reached the edge of the banks on Cliff Lake. He walked right on top of the tracks the two hunters had left. Soon, he found himself right next to the pile of coals. He knelt to examine the ground. Slowly tilting his head, he extended one had and felt the dirt. *One of them slept here*, he told himself.

Standing up, he walked around the other side of the fire. Kneeling again, he felt the ground once more. "And this is where the other slept," he said. Standing, Flint began to check all the tracks. He quickly learned that the men weren't leaving the way they had come into the Valley. He reached into his pocket, pulling out his map, and looking over all the options the men would have. If they were going to have to leave a different way, he knew they would probably take the rough Forest Service trail. Checking all the tracks through the camp, he eventually found where they had left it. Pulling out his compass, Flint checked the heading with his map. A smile crept onto his face, and he let out a slight laugh. *I may not even need to track them now if they are headed out on a trail. Well . . . that just made my day*, Flint said to himself as he began to walk out of the campsite.

Chapter 19

The Journey into Hell

Looking out over the swamp, Ethan turned his head and stared up toward the mountain next to them.

Vin gave Ethan a nudge, "It looks like an easy trail once you get up there."

"Sure, would be nice. I just don't know how in the hell I would have gotten you up there. Plus, we don't have time to go any other way," Ethan replied.

"Well, we can't pussyfoot around it anymore. Let's get this shit show underway," Vin said. Ethan adjusted Vin's arm around his shoulder and he stepped forward.

The ground lowered, and they had to step down into the swamp. The ground squished under their feet. Everything was wet. Ethan pulled Vin forward into long patches of thick, chest-high grass. Every step they took was worse than the one before. The ground was getting softer the farther they entered the swamp.

Vin moved his crutch forward, and the stick punched a hole into the ground, sinking deep into the mud. Falling to his right, Vin's left hand grabbed onto Ethan's shoulder, pulling them both over. The stick snapped in half, and they both crashed down into the mud. Mud splashed up around them as each man sank in deep. Ethan began to roll, trying to regain any sort of hold on himself. Not only had they sunk in the mud, but both were caught in a tangle of matted down grass that had gotten wrapped around them. After a few moments, Ethan was finally able to get his hands and knees under himself. Leaning up on his knees, he turned to help Vin. Vin had sunk deep on his right side and was trying to turn himself over to his back.

Ethan grabbed Vin, pulling him so he could sit up. Then, trying to make sure his feet didn't slip, Ethan made his way to his feet and began to pull Vin up. Vin slowly rose as Ethan continued to pull on him. Ethan's feet slipped out from under him, and this time, he fell backward, pulling Vin forward. As Ethan stumbled backward, he tripped on the grass, landing in the mud and sliding. Once he stopped, Ethan turned his head to realize he had just about slipped off the ground and into the water.

Stumbling up to one leg, Vin hobbled his way over to Ethan, trying to help steady him so that he didn't slide off the edge. "This is a damn shit show," Vin said.

"You saying I made the wrong call?" Ethan asked

"Nope, we don't know if the other ways would have been any better. You had to make a call, and you made one," Vin said.

"We're just going to have to lower our heads and power through. I doubt it will end up getting any easier," Ethan said.

"At least you stopped before you ended up in all of that shit," Vin said, pointing to the water.

Ethan paused, looking around. His hand went up to rub his forehead, pushing his hat up. "I don't think that really matters in the end. It looks like it runs directly in front of us, and we're going to have to cross through it anyway," Ethan said.

Vin took a deep breath and let out a sigh, "Well, then lead the way."

Shaking his head and smirking, Ethan squatted down, beginning a controlled slide off the ground and into the water. His eyes shot open as he gasped in shock. "Okay, yup it's pretty damn cold," he said. Ethan took a few steps forward to check how deep the water was, sinking up to his waist at its deepest point. "Alright, it's your turn. Let's get this over with," Ethan said.

Vin followed just like Ethan, squatting down and controlling his slide into the water. Once in the water, Ethan grabbed Vin and began to help steady him through it. The mud at the bottom was so soft that with each step they took, they would sink in up to their ankles.

The ground on the other side of the swamp didn't have tall grass. It was a flat clear piece of earth covered in grassy moss. The slow flowing water was freezing. Moving as fast as they could, they hurried to the other bank. "Alright, let me get you up there first." Ethan said.

Vin began to crawl up the side of the bank as Ethan push him up. Vin made it halfway up the bank when he began to slide back down into the water. Trying to grab a hold of anything he could, Vin's hands dug deep into the mud, but he was unable to get a hold of anything.

"Okay, we're going to have to try something different here," Ethan said. Squatting down, he submerged all except for his head into the water.

Vin placed his left foot into Ethan's hands.

"Okay, we're going to give it hell. Are you ready?" Ethan asked.

Vin looked at Ethan and nodded.

Ethan mustered all the strength he could, pushing through his legs and lifting Vin up. As Ethan lifted, Vin began to dig his hands into the bank as far as he could. Vin grabbed at anything he could just trying to keep his momentum going. Once Ethan's legs were fully extended, he began to lift with his arms and shoulders. As Ethan pushed up, his eyes slammed shut as pain seared through his shoulder. The strain of pushing Vin up the bank had opened his gunshot wound. Knowing he couldn't lose the momentum, it took everything Ethan had to fight through the pain. Vin dug his hands into the flat ground above the bank. With a final push from Ethan and digging his fingers into the bank, Vin was able to crawl his way out of the water and onto the flat ground.

Vin turned around and tried to help pull Ethan up out of the water as best he could. Ethan pushed his hands into the ground, trying to get his feet under him and out of the water. As he pushed off, his hands sunk into the mud halfway up his forearms. Moving his feet, his knees dragged through the mud, sinking his legs farther into the ground and causing him to trip over himself and splashing through the mud. Ethan struggled to get his feet under him. Once he finally did, he had dug himself into a hole past his knees.

Vin began to sit up. "So, I know you're a short son of a bitch, but you do seem a bit shorter than usual. Though, maybe you've always been able to go in the ball pit at McDonalds," Vin said.

Ethan turned to look at Vin. "That joke never gets old. If I were smarter, I would leave you here and haul my own ass out." Ethan said as he raised his right hand to flip Vin off.

Digging his way out of the mud hole he was in, Ethan tried to stay on top of the ground. Though with every step he took, he sunk past his shins. Walking over to Vin, Ethan proceeded to pull Vin out of the mud and up to his feet.

Vin wrapped his arm around Ethan's shoulder to help prop himself up. Vin had surpassed blinding pain of his right hip and rib cage. His entire body was completely shot. If he weren't being propped up, there would be no way he would be able to stay on his feet.

Ethan turned and looked at Vin as he got them ready to move. "Alright, you got your breath?" Ethan asked. Vin just nodded, signaling to get moving again. Ethan moved first, and his foot sunk deep into the mud. When Vin took a step, Ethan had to help pry him up out of the sludge. As Ethan moved Vin forward, Vin's weight sunk Ethan farther in — almost up to his knees. Ground water started to seep in around Ethan's legs as he once again found himself trying to pry his legs up out of the mud.

Hours passed by, and not only was Ethan dragging Vin through the swamp, but at this point he was also dragging himself through it. The sun had set, and they were moving in darkness as they reached the edge of the swamp. Ethan drug both of their bodies out of a pond of shallow water and onto the beginning of the solid ground. As they both made it securely out of the swamp, Ethan collapsed, falling flat on his face, and causing Vin to fall with him. Ethan was completely exhausted; he didn't want to move at all. He could feel his heartbeat in his fingertips and toes. Letting his body give out, it flattened under the weight of his pack and he let his face press into the ground as he closed his eyes. They both laid there, letting the time pass. The only movement out of either one was their chests moving in and out as they breathed. Until Ethan dug his hands into the dirt.

Sliding his hands close to his chest, Ethan pushed himself up to his knees. He turned his head over to look at Vin. Still the only movement was Vin breathing. Ethan closed his eyes. *We have come too far. I can't say we're close,' cause we aren't, but I have gotten us this far. I almost cracked for a minute back there. I can't let that happen again, and it will if I give up now. Keep your head down and keep moving forward,* Ethan said to himself. Looking at Vin, Ethan realized that they were both covered in mud and their clothes were soaking wet. *This could get a lot worse. I have to get us dry,* Ethan thought. He pushed himself to his feet and began to grab anything he could as he started to work on a fire.

When Vin opened his eyes, he was lying next to a fire and could once again see Ethan straight across from him. The last thing he remembered was falling to the ground as Ethan collapsed from exhaustion. The fall hadn't hurt because his body had already gone completely numb. He had been well past the point of exhaustion, having pushed his body to the point of hitting the wall. Then Ethan had dragged him over that wall. He went to push himself to sit up, but his arms gave out and he collapsed right onto his back. He let out a huge gasp of air.

"Just lie there, don't move. Just rest. I'm going to need your help to get you out of here, and you won't be able to help if you can't move," Ethan said.

Vin laid flat on his back. His body was forcing him to take huge deep breaths despite trying to slow his breathing.

"Just close your eyes and get some sleep. I'm standing watch." Ethan put two more logs onto the fire and picked his rifle up off the ground, scanning the area around them.

Vin wanted to speak up, wanted to take care of himself. He wanted to stand up on his own two feet and walk out of the mountains. But he couldn't do any of it. His body was completely giving up on him. He wasn't even able to hold his own head up any longer. His head lulled back on the ground, and his eyes fell shut.

It was almost mid-morning now, and Flint was still hot on their trail. Standing on the edge of the swamp, he weighed his options. Flint pulled out his map, looking over the choices the men would have to get back to their truck. *I can't believe they went this way. No way in hell would I have ever thought they would choose to go through a damn swamp*, Flint thought. Examining the paths, he knew they would have to get back on the main trail along the mountain eventually. *They won't be far past the swamp by now, if they even made it through it. I should easily be able to get in front of them now.* He turned and began heading back to where he would meet the trail once more. As he walked away, a half-smile broke on his face. *This will be perfect. All I have to do now is track down two weak and wounded animals. I'll be seeing them very soon.*

Chapter 20

Never Give Up

The sun slowly began to crack over the top of the mountain, shining down on Vin's face as the light broke at the peaks. The light hitting his face woke him. The first thing Vin saw upon opening his eyes was a smoldering pile of coals. That was all that was left of the fire. With the rest he'd gained, he was able to push himself to sit up. He scanned the side of the mountain over to the tree line of the forest. Nothing. He was alone. His heart began to race, and his mind wandered to all the possible reasons he was alone. Shifting himself in the dirt, Vin began to plan what he needed to do now.

"Hey! What the hell are you freaking out about, now?" Ethan yelled as he walked out of the trees.

Vin sighed in relief, "With the way things have been going on this trip, I was just assuming things were continuing to completely go to shit. I mean, that would just be par for the course," Vin replied.

Ethan began laughing as he walked back toward Vin.

When Ethan got back around the smoldering fire, he swung his rifle and pack off. Bending down to a knee, Ethan opened his pack. Shuffling through it, he pulled out one more power bar. Taking a second to look at it, he proceeded to hand it to Vin. "Eat up, you're going to need your strength. I want to cover some serious ground today," Ethan said.

Vin took the power bar and began to open it. Just as he was going to eat it, he stopped and looked back at Ethan. Ethan didn't have one for himself. "You not having breakfast?" Vin asked.

"That's it, man, it's the last of our food," Ethan replied.

"Wait, what?" Vin said.

"That's it, bud. Unless we find more food or I bring an animal down. After that power bar, we are out of food," Ethan said.

Vin stopped and covered the bar back up. "Then why are you just giving it to me? If we aren't going to save it, we should at least split it. You need to have something to eat as well," Vin said.

Ethan shrugged, "Dude, it's a damn power bar. It's going to take the edge off for a while, but that's it. You're in a lot worse of a way than I am. I'd rather give it to you. If there is anything to help give you the edge, then we need to do it," Ethan said.

Vin looked at the bar, analyzing the situation. Every moment of the trip flashed through his mind, settling on the hell that they had gone through. That's when the guilt began to settle in. He knew that if Ethan hadn't gone back for him then Ethan would have gotten back to the truck by now.

"Hey, hey, what in the hell are you thinking over there?" Ethan shouted.

Vin's attention shot back to Ethan, and he looked him straight in the eyes, "I think you should go on without me," Vin said. The tone of his voice was low and meek. It was the sound of a broken man.

Ethan barley acknowledging that Vin had even said anything. He just opened the water bottle that he had just filled and took a small sip.

"Hey, did you hear me? I want you to just hurry up and get the hell out of here."

Ethan ran his hand across his forehead.

"I'm serious! With as bad of shape I'm in, all you're going to do is end up getting us both killed. One of us is going to have to get out and tell people what we found here, and you are just going to have to come to terms with it. We aren't both going to get out of this one alive," Vin said.

Ethan adjusted his hat and placed the water bottle back in the pack, "You need to eat that power bar. It's going to be a long day."

"Are you not listening to me?" Vin shouted back.

Ethan stood up and swung his pack back on, holding his rifle in one hand. He quietly walked over to Vin. "You have got to be shitting me. I mean this must be a joke because, I'm pretty damn sure that the guy I've known since we could pee straight didn't just say he was willing to give up. The guy that I thought I was going to die of dehydration with when we were trying to hike our asses out of the west dessert without any water is now wanting to quit? Or are you telling me that battling my way back up that damn mountain and killing a psychopath, then dragging you back down it was all for nothing? And what in the hell was with that speech when I was about to give up? Yeah, you sure piped up and weren't ready to throw in the towel then. And if I dragged you through that nasty swamp for no reason, I'll kick your ass myself," Ethan said.

"Look, dude."

"No, you listen!" Ethan interrupted as Vin began to speak. Dropping to one knee, Ethan rolled up his pant leg then looked right at Vin. "Don't you ever expect me to leave you behind to die," he said pointing to his scarred leg.

Vin didn't know what to say, so they both just sat there in complete silence.

"The situation may have been different that day, but we still risked getting killed that time too," Ethan said breaking the silence.

"Wait a minute, that was completely different. Sure, you were in a bad way, but I wasn't. I was not anywhere near as bad off then as you are now. Physically, I could haul you out," Vin said.

"Are you kidding me? You have to be kidding me!" Ethan shouted back.

Vin stayed silent.

"Are you conveniently forgetting what happened?" Ethan asked.

Vin tilted his head down. "No, I'll never forget what happened," he murmured.

"We had just split up to head to two different glassing points,"

Vin began to shake his head, wanting to cut off the story.

"No, if you're expecting me to leave right now, then I'm going to remind you of how you didn't." Ethan said, undeterred. "I was over a mile away. You heard me scream and the gun go off. You sprinted the whole way with all your gear on, finding the exact spot, I was in." Ethan stopped for just a few seconds. "Anything ringing a bell yet?" He asked.

Vin put his hand over his mouth and softly spoke, "Yes," he answered.

"I walked right up on a grizzly bear with her cubs. I fired a shot, but it didn't do a damn thing. I was all but about to become a human happy meal when you showed up, firing a couple of shots, and scaring it off. I would have become bear shit if it weren't for you," Ethan said, pointing his finger right at Vin's chest. Both men sat there in silence for a few moments. Then Ethan finally stood up, "Now eat your damn breakfast then let's get your ass to your feet and get the hell out of here. We will crack that bottle as our last hoorah, but it has been sealed for eight years and still is, so we aren't giving up yet," Ethan said as he stood up, extending his hand toward Vin.

Looking up, Vin grabbed Ethan's hand. He let out a small exhale. It wasn't much, but a small spark had begun to burn again. Vin had broken, but luckily Ethan had picked him up and put the fight back in him. "Alright, let's give it hell," Vin said, pulling himself up.

Ethan propped Vin up as they got ready to move. Vin raised the power bar and took a bite. "Think this will be the last hoorah?" Vin asked.

Ethan paused. "I'm not going to lie, it seems more likely than not that it will be. But come hell or high water, we are going to make sure of that before we crack that bottle open that we have given everything that we could even imagine. We aren't going to lie down and die. We're going to go out with our boots on," Ethan said.

Vin didn't know what to say, so he remained silent, only able to muster a nod of his head.

"Well, then with that, let's get moving," Ethan said. Vin nodded again as Ethan took his first step forward, pulling Vin along with him.

As the men moved forward, pressing into the forest, a small rock slid off the trail higher up on the mountain, bouncing all the way down to the valley floor. Flint was squatting as he slowly lowered a pair of binoculars to his side, having finished watching the two men make their way into the cover of the forest. He examined his surroundings. Flint wanted to get in front of the men and set a trap, but in his current position there wasn't a clear route to get down off the trail, so he had just spent the night watching the men, checking their movements, and seeing what options they would end up having.

Besides, the more he watched them, the more he would end up learning about them. He hadn't expected them to go through the swamp, but he had never run into people like them before. Most people didn't fight back or even stick together. Throughout the years that he had been hunting people down, no other group or pair he had come across actually stuck together. At the first sign of trouble, everyone else had quit on each other, making a break for their own life. Every time, he would take one while the other ran. Once they were alone with the knowledge that someone was after them always caused them to panic. From there, the kill was easy.

But no one had ever come after him before. This was what he had been waiting for: for someone to finally show up and change the game. He knew their destination, and if he wanted to, he could always go and set his trap there. But the closer they got to their truck, the greater the chance they would end up running into more people. There was no way he was going to let that happen. For now, he'd just continue to stalk them. He had the ability to move faster than them, so all he had to do was keep pace and eventually the perfect trap would present itself. Flint stood up and stowed his binoculars, turning to once again trail the men.

Chapter 21

End of the Road

They pushed their way through the trees. The ground had begun to incline, and they were slowly gaining ground. As they journeyed up, they were coming close to the point where the trail would lower off the mountain. Even though they were almost there, it was getting late. The light had left, and darkness had completely overtaken the entire mountain range. Ethan dragged them both up to a flat point on the incline and stopped as the last of the light began to fade away. He lowered Vin down, sitting him next to the base of a tree. Vin wasn't moving except for light breaths of his chest; he had passed out from exhaustion hours before. Ethan set all their gear on the ground before dropping to the dirt and lying flat on his back.

Laying his head back on the ground, Ethan closed his eyes and tried to slow his breathing. *Just take a few seconds. Get some wind back in your lungs,* Ethan told himself. Though, he knew he still had things to do. The air felt different tonight than it had the previous two. The temperature had dropped, and with their clothes wet from sweating, they would be getting cold fast. A slight overcast was blocking any moon light.

Ethan let out one more giant sigh before hauling himself back onto his feet and starting his search for firewood. Once he had enough to get a small fire going, he built a fire pit close enough to Vin that he might begin to dry off. Ethan went back for more wood, then knelt by the fire to build it up more. Heat radiated from the flames, and he warmed his hands on it.

Turning, Ethan looked at Vin. He knew Vin had pushed beyond his limits for now. *This is just getting worse. Every day, things keep getting worse for him, and I'm not sure how long I can keep dragging him. Without any food, I can feel myself draining more and more,* Ethan told himself. Trying to weigh all the options and outcomes they had in front of them, reality was beginning to set in. It was only Thursday, and they told the girls not to worry until Sunday night. Then, to make things worse, it would be another half a day before search and rescue would get in the mountains, and then who knows how long it would take for someone to even come close to finding them. Without immediate help they didn't have a lot of time.

He felt the darkness of the night settling around him like a weight crushing his body. Ethan placed more wood on the fire then lowered his head and knelt by it. Folding his arms, Ethan closed his eyes. "I know it's been a while since I've been to church or formally said a prayer, but I always try to keep a prayer in my heart. I know you're up there and you're watching. We need help, and we need it bad. But I didn't expect to ask for this kind of help. I'm starting to see the writing on the wall. We're most likely not getting out of this one. If it comes to that, I just ask that you take care of the girls. They are going to need you to get through it. Just don't let them be alone, please. As for Vin and me, I don't know what you have written for us but," he paused for a few moments. Turning his head, Ethan opened his eyes and looked over at Vin before closing them again, "just please help us as far as you can." Opening his eyes, Ethan wiped a slight tear away. No matter what happened next, Ethan knew they would need all the help they could get.

As the night pushed on, the temperature dropped even more. Ethan did everything he could to build a big warm fire. Unless he was putting wood on the fire, he didn't move much, wanting to conserve as much energy as he could.

Higher up on the mountain, however, there was movement. Flint was hidden high above the men. He had spent a few hours sitting and watching one of them move around the fire before making a slow decent down the side of the mountain. He moved methodically, not making a single sound. Once he broke into the trees at the bottom of the mountain, the glimmer from the fire shown through like a spotlight. Moving from tree to tree, Flint crept silently through the forest. He was in no hurry, he had hours before the sun would rise.

Closing the distance, he saw the figures of the men cast in shadows from the fire, though he noticed only one was moving. Slowly, he changed his positioning to a different tree so that he had a clear view of both the men and the fire. One of them sat unmoving at the base of a tree, and the other had pulled a log over by the fire. The second man was awake, sitting in the dirt, and leaning his back against the log. The clouds had cleared off for the time being, so between the moon shining through the tree and the fire, it was bright enough for Flint to use his binoculars. Studying every detail he could, Flint scrutinized the men and their camp, making his plan.

Flint noticed that the unmoving man sitting at the base of the tree was the one he had taken, which meant that the one next to the fire was the one who had almost killed him. Flint's body began to tense and fill with rage. Lowering his binoculars, Flint pulled out his pistol.

Covering behind trees, he moved right to the edge of the tiny clearing. Leaning against a tree, he braced himself as he raised the pistol. The front sight leveled off right at the back his would-be killer's head. He began to pull the trigger backward. As the hammer began to cock, Flint suddenly released the trigger, lowered the gun back down to his side, and holstered it.

Flint raised his right hand, running it over his face. He was looking at the man that had almost killed him. *This one is personal.* The sadistic smile crept back on his face. Reaching over, Flint pulled out the tomahawk. He spun it in his hand once, then looked up. *I'm going bury this in his head.*

Ethan had settled by the fire, fighting to stay awake as his head bobbed down and his eyelids fell shut. He shot his head back up and forced his eyes open. *I need to stay awake and keep watch. I can't afford to fall asleep,* Ethan thought to himself. *I better get up and move around.* Pressing his hands against the log, Ethan pushed himself to his feet. Leaning back, he stretched his arms and brushed the debris from his pants.

Ethan turned his back to the fire and walked around the log. Studying the forest that he'd had his back to, his eyes shot wide open and his blood turned to ice in his veins. It felt as if his pulse had completely stopped as he realized that he was staring at a dead man. "No! I killed you!" Ethan shouted.

Flint was thirty yards from Ethan with his head tilted down, looking out of the top of his eyes with that smile firmly in place. Though this time, the side of the man's face was completely cut up. The man's stare burned holes into Ethan's brain. Then he saw that Flint had a tomahawk in his hand. Ethan turned, searching for his gun, but it was back leaning against the log. Turning back to face this psycho, Ethan saw that Flint had lowered his shoulders and began to charge at him.

The world turned to slow motion. Ethan knew he couldn't reach his rifle in time, so he lowered himself, placing one foot back. Tensing his upper body, he prepared for impact. This was going to end handto-hand. Twenty yards, then ten, then five. Flint had raised the tomahawk high above his head as he'd pushed forward. Shooting one hand up, Ethan grabbed the man's arm as they collided. The force caused Ethan to fall backward, landing them both in the fire. When they hit, both men rolled to the side, separating and extinguishing the flames that had caught on their clothing. For a moment, the two of them stood there, sizing the other up. Ethan peered deep into Flint's eyes expecting to see something, some form of human emotion, but there was nothing beyond a lifeless man with no remorse. His smile, however, hinted at a sadistic enjoyment.

With a quick sprint, Flint closed the gap to Ethan, wrapping his arms around Ethan's chest and knocking him backward. Ethan's back smacked against the ground, but he rolled with Flint's momentum, lifting his legs and launching the man off him and into the trees, away from the light of the fire. Racing back to his feet, Ethan peered deep into the darkness around him. A few seconds passed, but he couldn't see anything in the darkness. Flint had completely disappeared.

Turning a full circle, Ethan had no idea where the man had disappeared to. As Ethan turned, his rifle came back into his view, and his eyes widened. *Now, this my chance!* he thought.

Ethan lunged for the gun, grabbing it with both hands and taking the time to make sure there was a round loaded in the chamber. Ethan looked up in time to catch Flint come flying out of the darkness. Ethan raised the rifle across his body. Flint had gotten within arm's length just as the gun leveled in front of his face, and he swung the tomahawk forward. A clash of metal echoed through the air. The force of the tomahawk smacking into the side of the rifle rocked Ethan back onto his heels. Letting his arms give a little, Ethan pushed with his legs, forcing all his strength through his body and to his shoulders and arms. His push of the rifle forced the man to stumble backward.

As Flint tried to catch himself, he backed into Vin's unconscious body, knocking Vin to the ground as he fell backward over the top of him. Ethan brought the gun to his shoulder, and his eye quickly settled behind the rear sight. He tried to aim as the man fell to his back, but he used the momentum to continue the roll over his head. Flint's body became tangled with Vin's, and Ethan was unable to find a shot. Once he was away from Vin, Flint had made it to the fading light away from the fire. With only a quick view of the Flint's back, Ethan fired a shot into the darkness.

Ethan lowered the rifle and grabbed the bolt to eject the fired round. The bolt didn't budge. He tried to pry it open with all his strength, but nothing. It was jammed closed. He tried a second time. Nothing. Turing to the light of the fire he could see that the metal was smashed right where the tomahawk had hit the rifle. *Shit! Damn it! Come on, open, you son of a bitch!* Ethan pried on the bolt a few more times, but nothing could get it open. All he had now was an extremely heavy paper weight.

Throwing the rifle to the ground, Ethan reached behind his back, pulling out his field knife. Turning circles, he scanned for any movement or sound that would give away Flint's location, along with anything he could use as a weapon. His eyes stopped on his pack, they shot open. The second rifle *the stock is broken, but the firing mechanism is just fine,* Ethan thought.

Ethan took one step toward his bag and then froze. Flint stood just on the other side of the fire's flames, that sick and twisted look still smeared on his face. Ethan's eyes shifted toward the broken rifle, then back to Flint.

"Go for it . . . please . . ."Flint taunted.

Taking a deep breath, Ethan turned his body to face Flint.

"*AHHHHH!*" Flint let out a savage scream, raised his tomahawk over his head, and leaped straight through the fire.

Jumping back, Ethan swung his knife at Flint's chest. The blade sliced through Flint's old worn jacket and shirt, cutting open a gash on his chest as Ethan ducked out of the way of the tomahawk. They turned around, and Ethan now had his back to the fire. Flint touched a hand to his chest, seeing the blood on his fingers, he threw back his shoulders and puffed out his chest, the actions making him seem twice his size now in the dance of the fire's light, and Ethan could see that the wound was just filling Flint with even more adrenaline.

Flint slowly walked toward Ethan, showing no sign of hesitation or fear. Once he reached arm's length, Ethan plunged his knife at the man's chest. With a swing of the tomahawk, he knocked Ethan's arm to the side, then raised the tomahawk over his head and swung down.

Shooting his hand up, Ethan caught Flint's arm by the wrist. Flint drove down with all his might, and the tomahawk got closer and closer to Ethan's head. Knowing he was losing strength, Ethan swung the hand still holding his field knife back around, driving the blade into Flint's side just below his ribcage. A burst of air shot out of the man's lungs. Pushing Flint's arm away, Ethan began to pull the knife back out, but before he could, Flint punched Ethan in the side of the head with his free hand. The punch knocked Ethan off his feet. He fell backward, his head just barely missing the edge of the fire. Between the punch and the fall, Ethan was knocked into a daze.

Flint took a deep breath and ripped the knife out of his side, causing blood to pour out of the wound. Shaking his head back and forth, he regained his breath. Looking up, Ethan saw Flint stalking toward him. Digging his feet and hands into the earth like a crab, Ethan tried to push himself away, but he had forgotten about the fire, and as he slid back, the top of his head went right into the flames. The heat made his body shoot back down. Staring straight at Ethan, Flint dropped the knife and took two more steps forward. Keeping his eyes locked on Flint, Ethan began to push himself up to stand, but before he could get to his feet, Flint rushed forward and stomped him right in the chest.

Ethan laid on the ground, heaving and gasping for air. Flint walked over the top of him and stood with one foot on Ethan's chest, holding him down. Ethan watched Flint's fingers grip the handle of the tomahawk tighter and noticed that blood still oozed out of the wound on his side. With one sudden move, Flint dropped, slamming his knee into Ethan's chest. He swung the tomahawk above his head once again and drove it down. Both of Ethan's hands shot up, catching the man's wrist.

Ethan caught the look on Flint's face and the glare of the firelight on the metal of the tomahawk and knew that nothing was going to stop this man from killing him. As he fought as hard as he could, Ethan knew these would be the final moments of his life. With all his strength, Ethan fought the lowering tomahawk, but his arms were giving out, and it inched its way down.

Flint drew his free hand back and punched Ethan in the ribs. The sudden pain caused Ethan's arms to give slightly, and the blade dropped just a few inches in front of his face. The pain was excruciating, and Ethan was losing his strength as he fought to keep the blade from sinking into his skull. Flint's face lit up with excitement. Slamming his other hand on top of the tomahawk, he pushed with all his body weight down on Ethan. Ethan tried with every fiber in his body to push the blade away from his face, but it was futile. Inches turned to centimeters; centimeters turned to millimeters. The blade began to press against the skin above Ethan's eye. He could feel the pressure of the blade cutting into his head. The blade was so razor sharp that it sliced through the first layer of Ethan's skin like butter. He didn't even feel his skin being cut, only becoming aware of it because warm blood began to pour into his eyes, blurring his vision as it ran off the side of his face. He did everything he could to find more strength, but he had nothing left. Closing his eyes, Ethan accepted that this was the end.

There was a flash of light followed by a deafening noise.
Crack!

The pressure of the blade left Ethan's head, and all the weight left his chest. It took a few moments for Ethan to gather himself before wiping the blood from his eyes and turning his head to the side. Flint lay just a few feet away from him, flat on his back, his chest barely moving. Ethan rolled his head to the other side. He exhaled as comfort fell over his body.

Vin was lying on his side, holding the broken rifle.

Ethan didn't know what to say. Dragging himself up to a knee, then somehow gathering the strength to get to his feet, he walked over to Vin. He took the rifle then helped Vin sit up. Ethan turned to look at Flint. He was still lightly breathing. Vin tapped Ethan on the leg, "Remember . . . as long as we can breathe, we're not giving up," he said.

Ethan slowly nodded his head, then turned back to Flint lying there and walked over to him. Ethan stared directly into Flint's eyes. It was still there. Flint lay there fighting for life, and that sadistic look was still plastered on his face. Flint still held the tomahawk in his right hand. Looking over, Ethan could see the revolver Flint held the night he shot him. It had fallen on the ground. Flints left hand was outstretched, trying to reach for it. As his fingers fell just a few inches short, Ethan knew that if this man could muster any strength or find a way to say alive that he would attack them once again.

Ethan stepped on Flint's wrist, then bent down and ripped the tomahawk from his hand. Rotating it in the light, Ethan could see his own blood on the blade. Then he turned back to look at Flint, "I'm not going through this again." With one motion Ethan swung the tomahawk back, then drove it down, burying it deep into Flint's head. Walking back over to Vin, Ethan picked up the pack and buckled it to his chest. Vin extended a hand. Ethan grabbed it, pulling Vin up and wrapping his arm around his shoulders. "The trail isn't far, and we aren't stopping till we are out of these damn mountains," Ethan said.

It was extremely slow going. Hours had passed, and they had only made it a few miles. The sun had risen, but a thick cloud cover had settled over the mountain's valley. The temperature was dropping fast. Vin had almost lost all his strength, and Ethan was pretty much dragging him along by now. Ethan spotted a white flake falling. "Shit, we don't need right now," Ethan said. Vin tried to mumble something, but he was so delirious that Ethan had no idea what he said.

The trail was running flat along the side of the mountain, just a few feet above the valley floor, with the thick forest off to the other side. No matter how high the sun got, the clouds seemed to settle in more, and that single flake had now turned into a steady snow fall. The temperature dropping, and the snow had begun to stick to the ground. In fact, not only was the snow sticking to the ground, but it was sticking to both Ethan and Vin as well. Their torn and tattered clothes were beginning to soak through as the snow melted against their heated bodies. Ethan strained with all his might as he tried to push them both forward, but the snow fell faster and thicker with every minute that passed. The wind had picked up, blowing the snow right in Ethan's face. He turned his head to the side and squinted, trying to keep the snow from blinding him.

Ethan's foot slipped out from under him, and he slammed down to a knee, gasping in pain. Ethan checked on Vin, his head hung low and motion less. His eyes were shut, limbs were also lifeless and limp. There was just the slightest movement of his chest. *He's breathing, he hasn't given in yet. That means you can't either. Keep going, keep fighting.*
This isn't over! Ethan told himself.

He forced himself back to his feet and continued dragging both their asses farther down the trail. The snow was now ankle deep, and with the force of if, Ethan was now dragging Vin through the buildup. Pushing another step forward, Ethan stumbled again, and as he fell to a knee, Vin slipped, dropping him off the edge of the trail. Ethan clung to the arm that had been wrapped around his shoulder, but with Vin's weight and momentum, he was pulled headfirst off the side of the trail. The ledge wasn't high, they only fell a few feet, but in the horrific condition they both were in, their bodies weren't ready to handle the fall.

Ethan landed face down in the pile of snow. He lifted his head, seeing Vin lying just in front of him, securely on his side with his arm under his head. Ethan pushed himself up to his hands and knees.

What in the hell am I going to do? It will take everything I have just to get myself up to my feet. Can I really carry him any farther? Ethan asked himself. Leaning back on his heels, he turned back, looking up towards the trail. *It's just a few feet. Four days ago, I would have gotten up there without even breathing heavy.* Turning back, Ethan watched Vin lying there, barely even breathing. *I'll never get him back up there,* Ethan thought. Ethan crawled over to Vin on his hands and knees. Wrapping Vin's arm around himself, Ethan dragged him to the nearest tree. He pressed his shoulder against the trunk, pushing with his outside leg and using the trunk to leverage himself up to his feet.

Just keep moving forward, Ethan repeated to himself. Not being able to get back up to the trail, he pushed through the trees. He didn't even have the strength to stand up straight, and the snow in his face almost blinded him. Ethan took another step forward, pulling Vin along as he dragged his other leg up, but his supporting leg slipped out from under him once again, and they both face planted the snow. Ethan pushed himself to his hands and knees, letting his head drop as he looked at Vin. Ethan could feel his heartbeat pulsing through his entire body. Lifting his own arms had become a battle now. Frustration turned into anger. He couldn't give up now. After all of this he knew he would continue fighting to the end. *There is no way in hell I'm getting him back to his feet . . . I have to try though, Ethan* thought.

Ethan rolled Vin onto his back, then crawled to Vin's shoulders and, getting his feet under him, grabbed Vin under both his arms. Pushing with his legs, Ethan tried to drag Vin, but he only made it a few inches before his legs gave out once more. Ethan fell backward this time, landing on his butt. He pulled his pack off and slid over to the base of a tree. He looked at Vin, unconscious and barely breathing. Then looked at himself. *I can't do this. I can't even get to my own feet. It's time to admit the inevitable.*

Unzipping the pack, Ethan dug through it for a few moments before pulling out the bottle of whiskey. After years of going unopened on adventure after adventure with them, Ethan finally broke the seal on the bottle. He pulled the cork from the top and tilted his head back, take a long drink. The whiskey burned as it flowed down his throat, though it was barely noticeable with the pain he was in. He lowered the bottle to his side. Ethan couldn't remember the last time that he had eaten or drunk anything, and almost immediately he could feel a tingle in his fingers. His body began to relax for the first time in days. The tingle spread through his entire body, causing a slight warming sensation.

His mind began to wonder back and flash through his life. It started with adventures with his father and their group's first hunting trips. Adventures he and Vin had gone on almost played on repeat.

Then the flashes slowed down, he could see back to when he first met Ashley. Moving through the entire time he spent with her. The whiskey took more affect, and Ethan began to feel lightheaded. Flashes of a future he would never have began to overtake his mind. He could see his wedding to Ashley. Vin and Kasey were both there, right beside him and Ashley as best man and matron of honor.

A smile began to crawl across Ethan's face. "We were so close; we had a fair chance to get out of here." He turned and looked down at the bottle. "I wish I could have said goodbye, but I don't get to decide these things." Picking up the bottle again, Ethan took another drink. As he set the bottle back on the ground. The world began to fade away. "Well, give it hell or die trying," Ethan whispered to himself.

As his eyes drooped to a squint, his head fell back against the tree and rolled to the side. Dark settled around him, but his eyes focused in on a tiny bit of light. *There it is.* A slight smile grew on his face. *Go on, head for the light.* Ethan began to crawl, dragging the bottle with him. Five yards closer, then ten, then eventually twenty. The light had gotten bigger. The whole world had gone dark except for the light at the end of the tunnel. Then it flickered.

His eyes shot open. *It's a fire!*

"Help!" Ethan tried to scream, but his voice didn't carry through the wind. Leaning back on his heels, Ethan threw the glass bottle toward the fire as hard as he could. It smashed against a tree. He settled back as he saw movement, but the light was beginning to fade again. As he fell backward, Ethan saw someone running toward him and heard the words, "Get the horses, there are two guys back here! They look about dead! We have to get them help, now!"

Ryker Holmgren

Is a farmer in northern Utah and runs a small custom rifle shop. He is always seeking a new adventure. Whether it be hunting, fishing, or just exploring the back country.